Enslaved By The Ocean

OTHER TITLES BY BELLA JEWEL

Angels in Leather
Number Thirteen
Wingman
Life After Taylah
Precarious

MC SINNERS SERIES
Hell's Knights (MC Sinners 1)
Heaven's Sinners (MC Sinners 2)
Knights' Sinner (MC Sinners 3)
Bikers and Tinsel (MC Sinners 3.5)

Enslaved By The Ocean

Bella Jewel

Montlake Romance

This is a work of fiction. Names, characters, organizations, places, events, and incidents are either products of the author's imagination or are used fictitiously.

Text copyright © 2014 Bella Jewel
All rights reserved.

No part of this book may be reproduced, or stored in a retrieval system, or transmitted in any form or by any means, electronic, mechanical, photocopying, recording, or otherwise, without express written permission of the publisher.

Published by Montlake Romance, Seattle

www.apub.com

Amazon, the Amazon logo, and Montlake Romance are trademarks of Amazon.com, Inc., or its affiliates.

ISBN-13: 9781477825600
ISBN-10: 1477825606

Cover design by bürosüd° Munich, www.buerosued.de

Library of Congress Control Number: 2014907963

Printed in the United States of America

To my husband, my biker, my always and forever.

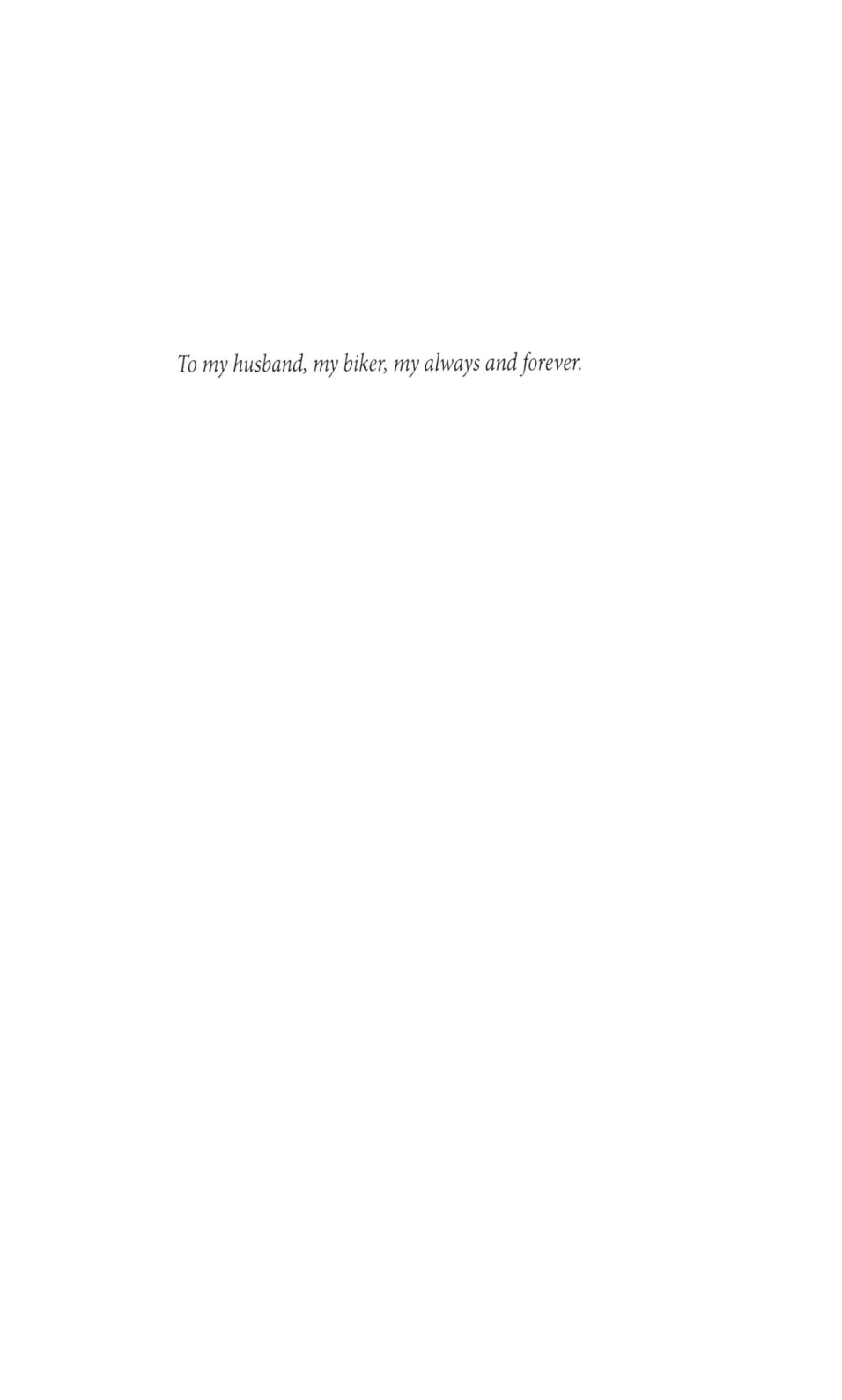

PROLOGUE

*If ye thinks he be ready to sail a beauty, then
ye better be willin' to sink with her!*

∼

"That's the way it's gonna be, little darling, we'll go riding on the horses," my father sings, his eyes soft and gentle. He stops after a moment, smiling down at me.

"Keep singing, Daddy," I beg, tugging the sleeve of his jacket.

"Princess, my sweet princess. I can't keep singing, I have to go." He smiles, his eyes crinkling at the sides.

"But why, Daddy?"

"Because sometimes daddies have to go away, and it's because they're protecting their daughters."

"I don't want you to go away," I cry, my eyes filling with tears.

He strokes my hair back from my face and smiles down at me. "You're going to be just fine. I raised a strong, beautiful daughter. Remember what I taught you, princess—always remember to find the good in the bad. Be caring and kind. Always know your place in the world, and most importantly, never let anyone hurt you. Not ever."

"Daddy," I cry as he stands, blowing me a kiss.

"Remember me forever, princess. Remember that on this day, in this moment, I love you."

"Daddy!" I wail again as he disappears into the darkness.

PRESENT

2011

My legs tremble as he nears the closet. I can hear his breathing; I can hear my own heart thudding. I clutch the gun, begging to the so-called god above to please let something happen so I don't have to use it. I don't want to use it. It's not in me. I'm not that kind of girl. It would haunt me forever if I was forced to take someone's life. Even someone like *him*. And he deserves it, God knows he does. I snake my tongue out, licking the coppery blood off my lip. It stings, and I clench my eyes shut, struggling to take a breath without making any noise. One noise and I'm dead.

I'm frightened.

I'm trapped.

And the only way out is through him, with a gun. A gun I don't want to use. I swallow, and I get the distinct taste of blood mixed with tears and saliva. My body shudders, and I force myself to stay steady. If he gets hold of me again, I'm dead. I don't doubt it. Not even for a second. He's a violent, angry, and aggressive man. I can't believe I ever thought he was the one for me. I can't believe I ever loved him. You just never see it coming. You never believe the person who holds your hand, the person who kisses you sweetly, the person who makes love to you on a rainy Sunday, will be the person to try and take your life.

"I know you're here, Indigo."

I'll never love my name again; not after hearing it coming from his lips. I clutch the gun, pointing it out and steadying my hand. The closet door swings open so suddenly I don't even get the chance to react. Cold blue eyes meet mine, and a slow sick grin spreads across a face I once loved. A hand lashes out, catching mine before I even get a chance to pull the trigger. I fight, though, God knows I fight. I screech, twisting my body as he pulls me out. A fist hits my jaw and I cry out, head spinning as I fall to the floor. The gun is still clutched in my hand, desperate fingers refusing to let go.

Then he's on top of me, more fists flying, one hand clutching the gun trying to . . . oh God . . . point it toward my head. I fight with every ounce of strength left in me. I fight until I can't breathe. I bring my knee up, and hit him right in the groin. Bellowing in pain, he slaps me so hard I see stars. His fingers wrap around my throat and I struggle to breathe as he forces my wrist to point the gun back toward my head.

I won't die like this—on the floor, like a pathetic animal. I won't. I can't. I kick again, twisting with everything I have. I manage to hit him in the kneecap, and he growls, losing his balance. It's all I need. I twist my wrist and point the gun toward his chest.

Then I pull the trigger.

And all I can see in the fading light . . . is red.

CHAPTER ONE

2013

Heaven, you fool. Did you ever hear of any pirates going there? Give me hell—it's a merrier place.

"Running doesn't solve anything."

My best friend Eric's voice fills my ears as I walk down the gravelly footpath to what is, I hope, a chance for freedom. I give him a quick glance over my shoulder, and he raises his brows at me. Eric is the perfect kind of man, really. He's smart, handsome in that "good boy" kind of way, rich, and overall a great guy. He's also very black and white. There is no in-between for Eric. Just how it is, or how it isn't. He doesn't like the idea of me running to another country. He wants me to stay, to fight, and to face my demons. It's easy for him. He doesn't have a crazy, angry ex stalking him.

"We've been over this, Eric," I say, jerking the heavy backpack on my shoulders. "I need to start again. I can't do that here."

"You can do that here . . ."

I spin around, tired of the same old conversation. Him trying to convince me it's better to stay and fight, yet not understanding how utterly terrifying my ordeal with Kane was. No one could possibly understand how terrifying that ordeal was, because they didn't live it. The months of going through court, seeing him after they put him away, living for the years that he was behind bars wondering if he'd somehow find a way to get out and find me. Then, counting down the hours until he was released, knowing he would seek revenge. The day he got out, I packed my bags and booked a ticket overseas. Last night, I received my first threatening phone call from him. That did it for me.

"I can't do that here," I snap. "You know I can't. I have no choice but to start again somewhere he can't find me. He will find me if I stay, and he will make my life hell."

"He's got a restraining order against him. He won't come near you."

I growl. See what I mean? Black and white. "Do you truly think that will stop him? Honestly, Eric, you think the law will stop someone like him seeking revenge, but it won't. It didn't stop him beating me within an inch of my life, and it won't stop him from doing it again."

"Running isn't going to solve this."

"No, maybe it won't, but it sure as hell is going to help. Are you with me, or are you not? I can do this alone, Eric, but you know I don't want to do that."

His eyes soften. Have you ever had that best friend who loves you? I have, my entire life. Eric will bend to me, no matter what I say. Most women would use that to their advantage. I don't. He's my friend, I adore him, but he's never going to be any more than that. I would never use him because of how he feels. In fact, it kind of frustrates me. He constantly sees me through rose-colored glasses, instead of seeing me for who I am, and my life for what it really is. He's put me on a pedestal, and damned if I can get down.

"I'm with you forever. You know that, Indi."

I nod, unable to be angry with him. I step forward, reaching out and gripping his shoulders. To most women, Eric is a very attractive man. Perfectly parted blond hair, brushed and slicked down. Eyes as blue as the sky. A long, lean body. Impeccably dressed. To them he's a dream. To me . . . he's too perfect. Call me adventurous, but I like them rugged.

Eric lifts his arms, wrapping his fingers around my elbows and smiling down at me.

"Can we just go, enjoy this trip, and then you can drop me off to start my life, and return to yours?"

"You know I'll miss you." He frowns.

"And I'll miss you, but we'll visit."

"It's not the same. We've been friends for so long."

"We'll be fine. Now come on, we're going to be late if we don't hurry."

I could have flown to London, the new place I have decided to live in. I can't really say why I chose London—I guess it came down to the fact that I really wanted to escape the US for a while. So, instead of flying, I decided to hire a small yacht that goes directly across from the United States to the United Kingdom. I want the chance to unwind, relax, take a break, and then get off the ship, ready to recreate my life. Eric decided to come for the ride with me, needing to sort out some business in London. He's a massively successful business owner and has clients all over the world. It was a great excuse for him to make some face-to-face visits.

There's a cool morning breeze chilling my skin when we arrive at the small yacht on the wharf. I find myself smiling at the entire situation. I haven't been on any type of boat for such a long time. There's a man waiting, a man I paid good money for, and he smiles when he notices us. As we get closer I see he's an older gentleman, with graying hair and dark brown eyes. His skin is well worn from the sun, but he looks friendly. When we stop in front of him, he stretches his hand out. I take it. "Hello, and welcome to my yacht, The Dreamer. Thanks for considering me for your adventure. I'm John. If you'll step on board, I will show you around."

"Thanks, John." I smile. "I'm Indigo, and this is my best friend, Eric."

Eric reaches out and shakes John's hand. "Nice to meet you, John."

John nods and we head onto the yacht. I'm quite surprised. I ordered a small yacht, yet it's actually quite substantial on board. I'm fascinated to know what a large one looks like.

This yacht is long, sleek, white, and extremely well looked-after. We step on board, and I peer around. The deck is rather large, outfitted with sun lounges and tables and chairs that are bolted to the floor. John walks us toward the cabin that goes below deck, and we follow him down when he opens the big, glass door.

It's quite large inside. It has a basic living area, with a lounge and a small television. There is a little kitchen and a basic bathroom and toilet. At the end there are two rooms: one for me, and one for Eric. John sleeps on deck in his little navigation office. Each room has a double bed, and both look very luxurious. John has it set up for comfort, and I feel myself relaxing for the first time in months.

"This is basically it," John explains. "There is loads of food in the fridge and cupboards. There are fresh towels and linens in the cupboard in the left room. Feel free to laze about on deck. I will be in my navigation office most of the time, so just let me know if you need anything. Otherwise, the space is all yours."

"Thank you, John." I beam.

He tips his hat. "We'll be taking off now. I ask that you stay below deck until we do."

"We will. Thank you." Eric nods.

"Oh, one last thing. In case of emergency, there is a lifeboat on the side of the yacht. It's easy to get down: you just step in and pull the chain. The boat contains life jackets which you can slip on and pull the little red lever to inflate."

We both nod, and John smiles before disappearing up on deck. Eric turns to me, grinning and rubbing his hands together. "Where do we start?"

I smile, and turn, running off toward the biggest room. "I claim this!" I squeal.

"Oh!" Eric yells, chasing me. "No way!"

We both leap onto the large bed at the same time, laughing and rolling onto our backs.

"You sure about this?" Eric suddenly says. "There's no turning back now."

I nod, rolling toward him. "I'm sure. I want this, Eric."

"I know, but I'm your friend . . . I have to triple check."

I smile at him, reaching out and curling my fingers through his. "I know you are, but this is the best thing for me right now."

"And if he finds you over there?"

"Eric," I warn. "Please don't. I have to believe I can change my life and escape him."

"Of course," he says, shaking his head. "I'm sorry."

"I am going to be fine. I've lived through so much . . ."

He squeezes my hand. "You have. For a girl your age, you're super tough."

I laugh softly, but his statement isn't so far from the truth. I have had a hard life. Once, a long time ago, I had a nice happy family. A mom, a dad—hell, even a dog. Then it all changed. My dad started going funny and disappearing all the time. He and Mom would fight so often I forgot what them talking sweetly sounded like, and then one night he just left and I never saw him again.

I know my daddy was a bad man. Even back then I knew, but I loved him. My mom got sick two years after he left, and she died. Eric was always my friend, and managed to keep in contact with me, even when I got shuffled through foster homes. Then I met Kane. He was my foster brother in my last home, he was older than me, but I fell for him hard and fast. We moved away, and I thought things were good—until he started beating me.

Then that one night I snapped, and here I am . . .

"I just need this, you know?" I whisper, shifting closer to Eric.

"Yeah," he says, nodding. "I know."

And we leave it at that.

Because there really is nothing else to say.

We spend the rest of the day just chilling out. Eric falls asleep in the afternoon, so I head up onto the deck and over to John's navigation office. I'm about to step in when I hear him on the radio.

"Are they still in these waters?"

The radio crackles, and a voice can be heard over it. "We haven't seen them, or picked them up, but there was a sighting."

"I'll turn my radar on, just to make sure they come nowhere near my yacht. I have guests, and I don't need pirates jumping into the picture and making this a trip they won't want to remember."

Did he just say pirates?

He turns and sees me at the door, and quickly ends the call.

"Did you say pirates?" I ask, a little confused.

"I did." He sighs. "Unfortunately, we have occasional problems with them."

"As in 'arrrr' pirates?"

He looks confused. His eyes narrow and he shakes his head slightly. "Yes."

"I thought they were fictional?"

He smiles a little. "No love, they're certainly not fictional. The word *pirate* is more the fictional part. There've always been groups of them on the ocean. They come out here to do illegal business, given that the laws are very different in certain areas."

"I don't . . . quite understand. I thought they weren't real."

"Of course they are, and they cause a lot of problems."

"Is there a problem now?"

My heart is hammering, and I feel a little nervous.

"We should be fine. There has just been a sighting, but the navy is certain they've turned them around."

I swallow and nod.

God, I hope so.

～

The sea spray hits my face, and I groan with delight. I love the smell of the ocean; it's something I don't think I'll ever get sick of. It's day two, and we've been taking our time. Eric and I have enjoyed every second. We've spent hours in the sun drinking beer, we've feasted on fresh fish and prawns, we've slept, and we've even swum once. It's been so relaxing and perfect. It's just what I needed, and by the looks of Eric, lounging on the sun lounge, it's been just what he needed, too.

"You look comfy," I say, walking over and dropping down beside him.

"I am," he yawns.

The sun is just setting over the horizon, and the cool evening air is coming in. I lie back on the other lounge and sigh deeply.

"God, I don't want to go back to work," he murmurs.

"No," I moan. "I don't want to find a place and think about life again."

"At least it's in a new place. It'll be fun."

"Truth," I yawn. "I'm hungry. I could use a big juicy steak right about now."

Eric grunts. "You're such a man sometimes."

"Hey," I giggle. "It's perfectly okay for women to like meat."

"Yeah," he laughs. "Maybe John has some for us."

"He has everything in the fridge. The man is well worth the money I paid."

"You should sing to him, make it worth his while doing all this for you," Eric jokes.

"Hey," I say. "I paid him very well. And besides, I can't sing."

"Lies," he murmurs. "Your voice is like an angel's."

I close my eyes with a smile and stretch, sighing deeply. I've been singing for a long time, and have always had comments on how good I am, but it's not something I ever wanted to take further. Pushing it from my mind, I roll to my side and soak up the sun. I'm just about to drift off into a late afternoon nap when Eric's sunlounger creaks loudly beside me.

"Do you smell that?" he says.

I take a deep breath in and scrunch my nose. My eyes flicker open.

"Smells like . . . smoke?"

"Yeah, it does."

Suddenly he's on full alert, looking around. His eyes widen, and he quickly gets off his lounge. I turn, concerned, and see a puff of gray smoke coming from downstairs.

"John!" Eric yells.

John comes rushing out of his office just as the yacht's alarms sound. With wide eyes, John swings the door to the cabin open and rushes down. Eric and I both run over just in time to see him open a passage at the back of the yacht. Thick gray smoke pours out, followed by flames.

"Oh God," I whisper, clutching Eric.

"Get in the lifeboat," John yells, running back up toward us. "The engine is on fire. I had someone work on it recently because it was playing up. I thought it was fixed—I'm so sorry. It's very dangerous. If it breaks into the gas line, it'll blow. I need to get you both to safety before I see what it is."

Without an argument, Eric and I run toward the lifeboat at the edge of the yacht. We climb in and pull the chain as instructed, and the boat lowers. When we hit the water, Eric uses the paddles to push us a little away from the yacht. As we float, eyes wide, we watch John running around frantically with his radio. He's calling "Mayday, mayday," and we both know that means emergency.

"Should we get him off the yacht?" I ask, frantically.

"No, he knows what he's doing," Eric says, gripping my hand.

"I'm scared, Eric."

"It will be okay, it's probably just an engine . . ."

We hear a loud boom, and then we see the smoke thicken. John rushes down, and Eric stands quickly, yelling for him to stop. He doesn't. He goes below deck and then, for the longest moment, we hear nothing.

"We should go back," I cry, standing too.

"No," Eric says, gripping my shoulder. "If it blows . . ."

"We can't leave him in there. That smoke will kill him!"

Eric spins, gripping my shoulders. "It's his yacht. He knows what he's doing. We can't go in there."

"But . . ."

"If it blows," Eric yells, "we die."

"If we leave him there, *he* dies!"

"Indigo, there's nothing you can do right now. Getting in his way will only cause a problem."

I drop back down, wrapping my arms around my stomach and trembling. I feel sick. How did we end up here? Five minutes ago, we were chilling and enjoying the afternoon. Now, we're sitting in a rescue boat, wondering what the next few minutes will hold.

"Hey," Eric says, dropping down beside me. "It's going to be okay. He's probably just going to put the fire out and wait for help."

"He hasn't come back out."

"He will."

I stand, shaking. I was taught never to leave someone behind, and I can't just sit here and wait. It's not right. He could be hurt.

"I'm going to get him. He could be passed out, or worse . . ."

"No," Eric says, gripping my arm. "It's dangerous."

"I'm not leaving him, Eric!" I scream. "This isn't your choice to make."

I lunge forward, and that's when it happens. The explosion. I'm just gripping the paddles to row back toward it when we hear the ear-shattering blast. Flames roar out from below deck, and black smoke fills the sky. I know I'm screaming, and I know Eric is pulling me back as I try to fight forward. I squirm in his arms, begging and panting. Fire roars up onto the deck, and right before our eyes the yacht begins to crumble. How can something burn down in the middle of a bed of water? It's cruel.

"Please," I rasp, cupping my ears as they begin ringing. "Eric . . ."

"He's gone," he whispers. "He couldn't have survived that. Indigo, we have to paddle away. If that thing blows more . . . we die too."

"Help will come," I whisper, shaking. "We can't go far."

"We have to row!"

"No, Eric!" I scream.

"Indigo, look at me!" he yells, spinning me around. "You have to trust me right now."

"He could be alive!"

"Do you see those flames?" he bellows. "He's not alive."

"Eric!" I scream.

He pulls me down and into his arms, tucking me into his chest. "You have to trust me. Hush, Indigo."

I close my eyes, and tears stream down my face. It hurts. It hurts so badly I want to throw up. My entire body shakes, and I clutch Eric like he's the only thing keeping me alive. I guess right now he is. I hear more small explosions, and I squeeze my eyes more tightly shut. I don't want to open them. I can't. I just hold on to Eric and try to push out the horror happening right in front of me.

Eventually, that horror becomes too much.

I black out.

CHAPTER TWO

Yo ho! A pirate's life for me.

Two days we're on that water; two long days. Eric made the mistake of rowing us too far out, and we lost sight of the yacht. We waited each day for a chopper, or a rescue boat. None ever came. We floated, with no food, no water, and no sun protection. My skin began to peel off at the end of the first day. Eric gave me his shirt to try and cover my skin, but I ended up giving it back when I saw his skin beginning to blister.

Two days without water in the blazing sun, and my throat is sore, dry, and burning. My body is weak. My skin is burned. My heart aches. I'm frightened, for my life and Eric's. We have no escape. Unless someone finds us . . . but what if they don't? Oh God, what if this is it for us? I don't want to die like this. It's not how it's meant to go. I'm meant to grow old, and have children. Not become a rotting bag of bones on a stranded boat in the ocean. We have my phone with me, but it has no service out here, not to mention the battery life is minimal.

On the evening of day two, Eric and I are curled together, trying to protect each other from the cool evening breeze, when suddenly the boat begins to rock. It's only a light, gentle rocking, but it's movement. We both lift our heads to see a mass of lights coming toward us. It's a ship. It has to be. We both bolt upright and get to our feet, our legs wobbling. My heart begins to thump. Oh God, is it a rescue ship? Are we saved? The relief that floods my system, as I lift my hands and start yelling in a croaky voice, is huge.

"Is it a ship?" Eric rasps, his voice dry and crackly.

My eyes burn from too much salt and too little water, but I squint and as it comes closer, I can see it is. "Yes."

"I know," he croaks. "But what kind of ship?"

"Does it matter?"

He grunts angrily. The last few days haven't been easy on our friendship. When faced with life and death, anyone would become overly stressed. I drop to my knees, feeling my heart hammer. This is our chance to get help. We've been out here two solid days and there's a ship heading in our direction. I won't be letting it pass. Eric moves about, and our tiny lifeboat rocks. I lift my sore, aching arms and begin flashing the little light from my life jacket.

Suddenly a large light turns and points in our direction. I squint and cover my eyes. They've seen us. Help has arrived. Oh God, we're going to survive this. My knees buckle and I fall, relief flooding me. Eric continues to yell and wave the flashlight around. From this angle, the light isn't piercing my eyes, and so I can see what he can't, and when I see it, my blood runs cold. It's a flag . . . but it's not a country flag, or a navy flag. No . . . it's a skull and crossbones. My stomach lurches, and it takes me a moment to gather my bearings enough to reach for Eric's leg and pull at him, bringing him down to my level.

"What the hell, Indi?"

"Th-th-th-the . . ."

"What's wrong?" he asks, confusion washing over his features.

"Th-th-the flag. They're pirates."

"What?"

"John said . . . he said . . . there were pirates out here. Oh God, Eric, they're pirates."

He shakes his head in confusion, so I lift my wobbling hand and point toward the ship that's now coming closer. His eyes narrow, and then I see fear fill his eyes. He reels backward, fumbling for something to paddle us away. Anything to get us out of here. Deep down in my terrified soul, I know we'll never outrun a ship like that. We have only two options—jump overboard, or let them capture us. Right now, both could possibly mean death; it's just a matter of which death we want. Maybe they won't hurt us. Maybe they'll just let us go, or leave us here?

No. They're pirates. Everyone knows that's not how it works.

I clutch Eric, terrified. My heart is beating so heavily it hurts, and my body is tingling all over. Fear and panic wash through me. The urge to flee, to run, and to save myself is huge . . . yet there's nowhere to run to. Eric's eyes are darting, and he quickly flicks the flashlight off. His body shudders and for a long moment, all we can see is darkness. Our breathing is the only sound I can hear until the ship comes closer, and waves begin to lap against the boat. My heart hurts. It aches so badly I want to rip it out just to stop it. This is like a nightmare, except I can't wake up. I can't do anything but pray to God these pirates aren't awful.

"We should jump over," Eric whispers.

"And die?" I hiss.

"We're going to die if they get hold of us!"

"We can't be sure of that."

"It's too dangerous!" he growls.

I can't answer, because the light swings our way and falls directly on our boat as the large ship stops beside us. I can't see a damn thing; all I can see is the blinding light. I hear voices, and then I hear the sounds of ladders rolling down. I whimper, and clutch Eric closer.

I clamp my eyes closed, wanting to drown it all out, wanting to take myself away from this fear. I feel Eric flinch, and then I hear the ragged, angry voice fill my ears.

"Get on the ship."

The raspy, deadly voice causes ice to run through my veins. I open my eyes and see a man hanging off the ladder, glaring at us.

"Please, we don't want any trouble," Eric whispers.

"Shut up. Get on the fuckin' ship."

"Just leave us here, we're just . . ."

The man pulls out a long, rusty sword and thrusts it toward Eric's face. He yelps and leaps backward, knocking me over. I cry out as my sunburned back hits the side of the boat.

"Get on the fuckin' ship. Now."

Eric puts his hands up, trembling. "Okay, okay."

He wobbles as he edges toward the ladder. The pirate grips his arm, hurling him over until he's dangling like a floppy dog off the ladder, one hand grabbing it desperately. His screams rip through me, and I wrap my arms around myself. The pirate shoves at him, forcing him to climb the ladder, and then he turns to me. He's an older man, with a long, bushy beard and thinning gray hair. He crooks his finger, and I don't dare argue. I walk forward, reaching out and taking the ladder in my hands. He grips my shoulder, causing me to cry out as his fingers cause my burned skin to protest angrily. He keeps hold of my shoulder as we climb, and when we step over the side he shoves me forward.

I crash into Eric, hard. He wraps protective arms around me, and I'm grateful. I blink my eyes, letting them adjust to the twenty or so men surrounding us. I let my gaze scan them all, and I'm surprised to find them . . . clean. Well, they're not clean as such, but they're certainly not fat, dirty pirates like I would have expected. It doesn't make them any less deadly, though. Every one of them has a hard, angry expression. They all hold weapons of some sort.

Swords. Knives. Guns. I tighten my grip on Eric and watch the older man, the one who grabbed us, walk toward the door that goes down below deck. He flicks it open and yells down.

"Cap'n. CAP!"

Wait. He's not the captain? I swallow, and I feel Eric flinch beside me. I get a quick glance of the massive ship, but I don't take a great deal of notice. My body is too terrified. The old man turns, walks over to us, and stops, sword out, ready for action. He leans down, letting his eyes scan over both of us, as if weighing up whether we should live or die. Then his eyes harden and he growls, "Get on the fuckin' floor."

"Please," Eric pleads.

The man shoves the sword toward Eric's throat, slicing a line just thin enough to cause a trickle of blood to fall. I drop to my knees, terrified. Eric drops beside me, hand clutching his throat, his eyes wide with shock.

"Head to the floor!" The pirate barks.

We both lower ourselves until our heads touch the dirty, smelly deck. Then we just lie there, waiting.

"Where you from?" The pirate asks, a moment later.

"A . . . A . . . America," I rasp.

He chuckles, and I peer up enough to see him turning toward the door. I hear the sound of boots, and then I see the door creak open. I close my eyes, turning my face toward the ground. I can't face this. God, what if they rape me? Or slowly torture us? Or sell us? There are so many ways this could go. I hear the deck creak as the captain walks toward us. When that creaking stops, I hold my breath. Is this it? Will he just raise his gun and shoot us? Perhaps he'll cut us, and throw us overboard to bleed out?

"Where the fuck did you get these two?"

His voice . . . it's so . . . young. I want to look up, but my body is frozen with fear.

"They were on a boat, screamin' and carryin' on."

"They alone?"

"Yeah, just the two of them."

It's silent a moment, and I hear Eric shuffle beside me before attempting to speak. "We were on a cruise and . . ."

"Did I give you permission to fuckin' talk?" the captain barks.

Eric flinches again, and promptly stops speaking. Silence fills the air, and all I can hear is my own ragged, terrified breathing.

"You, look here."

Oh God, he's talking to me. Hot tears fill my eyes and I slowly raise my head. What I expect to see and what I actually see are two very different things. It takes me a solid moment to realize that the man I am looking at is actually a pirate. In my head, I had an image of an old, smelly man . . . but him . . . oh, God . . . he's breathtaking. Even in my fear, I can't move my eyes from him. It's impossible to look away. It's impossible to believe that somebody so beautiful would be in a place like this.

He's tall; that's the first thing I notice. His large, six-foot frame would overpower most men. He's a mass of solid muscle, and his large arms are covered in black Celtic tattoos. He's wearing a pair of ragged, black jeans, a gun and sword belt, and a black singlet that stretches across his large, chiseled chest. I can see a mass of thick, long black hair peeking out from under the red bandana he wears on his head. When my eyes settle on his, I suck in a deep, raspy breath. They're so dark they look black, yet they're so utterly beautiful and captivating. His face is covered in stubble, and he's got jewelry in both his ears. A thick, gold chain hangs around his neck. He's dazzling, but like the rest of them, he looks incredibly deadly.

For the longest moment he holds my gaze, until finally he speaks. "What are you doin' out on the ocean?"

I swallow and open my mouth to answer, but my voice doesn't want to work.

"Answer me, girl," he barks.

"We were on a yacht," I croak. "It caught fire and we got on a lifeboat, but Eric . . . I mean . . . it drifted away and we ended up trapped."

He reaches up, running his fingers over the dark stubble on his cheeks. The older pirate steps up beside him and leans down, whispering something in his ear. The captain's eyes widen, and he turns his gaze to me, letting his eyes slide up and down my body. Nodding, as if impressed, he turns and says something to Old Man Pirate, and they both nod.

"You, come here," he says, crooking his finger at me.

Eric lashes out, gripping my wrist as I move to get up. "She's not going anywhere near you."

The captain turns his gaze to Eric, and then lifts his hand and clicks his fingers. Two pirates appear behind Eric, and one of them hits him so hard his face is smashed into the deck. I get to my knees, crying out and reaching out for him. A hard set of arms curl around mine and pull me back. I watch as two pirates lift Eric, one on each arm, and begin dragging him toward the large door leading down to the lower deck.

"Let him go. Please!" I beg.

I'm spun around until I'm facing the captain. His fingers dig into my shoulders and I cry out, squirming.

"Shut your fuckin' mouth and walk."

He shoves me forward, and I force my legs to move, even though they feel like they're filled with lead.

"Where are we takin' the boy, Hendrix?"

Hendrix. Hendrix. *Hendrix.* That's his name?

"Take him to the holding cells. I'll deal with him soon. I'm takin' the girl first. Need some info outta her."

Info. What sort of info? Why would he want info out of me?

I feel his hand push my back again, and I don't dare argue. When I reach the large door, I peer down. Old, wooden stairs are all I can see. I take a step, and then another, and another, until I'm at the bottom. I peer around the large ship, quite surprised at its size. The first level basically consists of a long hall with doorways branching off from each side. I am shoved again, so I take another step. As I move down the halls, I catch a glimpse of the small bunk rooms on the side. I see a large room through one of the doors that seems to be a dining hall. I reach a shut door at the end of the hall, and Hendrix reaches around me, gripping the handle and flinging it open. He shoves me, and I stumble forward.

I manage to gather my footing before I fall. I get a chance to peer around. This must be his room. It's large with dark wooden walls, a toilet and shower off to the side, a large bed in the middle, and a desk near a set of windows at the back. Hendrix shoves me again, so I continue to walk forward until I reach a small sofa. He grips my shoulder, forcing me down onto it. I don't fight him. My mind is screaming at me to just go along with it. He might not kill me if I do as I'm told. I think about Eric, and my heart clenches. Is he okay? Are they hurting him right now? I can't not ask. I can't just forget about my friend.

"Are they hurting him?" I croak.

Hendrix is standing in front of me, and at my words he kneels. He grips my wrists and holds them tightly in his hands, making it impossible for me to move. Our eyes meet, and I flinch. There's so much behind those eyes, so much pain, so much anger, so much death . . .

"What is goin' on with him ain't your concern. What is your concern is survivin'. You do as I ask, you live. You don't, you die. It's simple."

Simple. *Simple.* Of course, it's so freaking simple. I put my head down, swallowing over and over to stop the bile rising in my throat.

"How old are you, girl?"

"My name is Indigo," I snap, lifting my head to meet his glare.

"Don't fuckin' care what your name is; it don't matter to me. I asked how old you are."

"What does it matter?" I whisper. "If you're going to rape me, I don't imagine you'll care."

He snorts. "No, I suppose I won't. Answer me anyway."

My body goes stiff.

"Now," he growls.

"I'm twenty-four."

He narrows his eyes, and nods his head. "You fucked many men?"

Oh. My. *God.*

"Fuck you," I spit.

He lifts his hand, and he slaps me so hard I see stars. My body stiffens, and just like that I crumble. My moment of strength crawls back to my inner depths and stays there.

"Answer my fuckin' question, or I'll chain you up in the cell with the rats."

"No," I croak.

"No you haven't fucked a lot, or no you won't answer my question?"

"No I haven't fucked a lot."

"Good."

Good? I raise my head, meeting his gaze with a powerful glare.

"Who are you?" I rasp.

"Someone you don't want to fuck with."

"W . . . w . . . w . . . what do you want with me?" I say in a small voice.

He grins, and it's not nice. His eyes are so full of threat. I shudder, but when he speaks, my entire world stops.

"I want to sell you."

Oh.

God.

He wants to sell me. I can't even breathe through that. My entire body is tingling, and my head spins. He wants to sell me? Like . . . a sex slave? Or on the black market? I lift my head, and my eyes burn as I stare into his. "You want to sell me?" I gasp.

"I don't want to sell you," he growls, turning his gaze away from mine and standing. He walks over to his desk and picks up a cigarette, lighting it. "I *am* selling you."

"Why?" I whisper.

"Because I owe someone, and you're the perfect payment. He likes girls like you."

Girls like me. Oh God. I don't want to know what that means.

"P . . . p . . . please, just let me go. I'll leave . . ."

He snorts. "No can do. I really do need to settle that debt. Don't worry, he's only mean when you piss him off."

"I won't let you do this," I yell, my body shaking.

He storms over, grips my shoulder and hurls me up to my feet. I scream in pain as his fingers dig into my skin. "You have no choice. You will learn I am not the sort of man you want to play with. I will crush you. Now, turn around."

"What?" I whisper.

He lunges forward, gripping my shoulder and spinning me. "Don't argue, just do."

He begins patting my sides. He's looking for weapons. He's going to find my phone. My only chance of escape. When his fingers go over my pockets, he shoves his hand in and pulls out my cell phone. "You ain't keepin' this."

"Please, just let me go."

He spins and glares at me, before turning and walking over to the door. He opens it, sticks his head out and bellows, "Drake!"

A moment later, a tall, blond pirate with a jagged scar running from his temple to his mouth down the left side of his face walks in. He doesn't look at me; he simply stands at the door waiting for orders. He's huge, with broad shoulders and muscle beyond that of a normal man. Hendrix shoves me toward him, and I smother the terrified scream escaping my throat.

"Put her in the cells. Let's show her what kind of people she's playing with."

"Please," I beg.

"I suggest you learn to close your mouth unless you're being spoken to," Hendrix snarls. "I will put you in your place, girl. Don't doubt it. Your begging, it means nothing to me."

My lip trembles, and I drop my head.

"Now, put your arms behind your back."

I snap my head up. "What? No."

Hendrix growls, spinning and stalking over to his desk. He pulls out a set of handcuffs, and with a determined glare he walks over, grasping my shoulder and spinning me around.

I decide this is my moment to fight. I swing my leg backward, hitting him in the kneecap. He bellows, but his fingers don't leave my shoulder. He slams me forward, pressing me against the wall. I squirm and kick, twisting my body in a poor attempt to escape his hold. Suddenly, there's a cold, hard item pressed against my temple.

"It's simple," he hisses into my ear. "You do as I ask, or I blow your brains out. Either is fine with me. You choose right now to live or die. What's it going to be?"

"It doesn't matter either way," I cry, squirming.

"Live or die?" he roars, pressing me harder into the wall.

"Live!" I scream. "Live!"

"Then shut your mouth, and do as you're fucking told," he snarls.

He removes the gun, and my knees threaten to give way. I am shaking all over, and my teeth clatter together. Hendrix pulls my hands behind my back, causing a pained cry to leave my throat. Then he snaps on a pair of handcuffs. He spins me around, and our eyes meet for a moment. There has to be something else in there. Surely this can't be everything? He is acting like a monster, but there's a depth to his eyes that says otherwise.

"Please, let me have some water," I whisper.

"Do you think this is a fucking luxury holiday?" he snaps.

"I'll die, and then you won't get your sale."

His eyes flicker with shock for a moment, and then they go hard. "Don't threaten me again, girl."

He shoves me toward the blond man, and he takes hold of the chain linking the cuffs together and tugs. I can do nothing but obey. Like a naughty puppy, I follow him down the halls.

As he leads, I take in my surroundings. Most of the doors to the left and right of us are closed, so I can't see inside them. There's a large room right at the end to the left, and I can hear noisy voices and music coming from it. We reach the end of the hall, and there's an old, broken wooden door. Blondie opens it and shoves me down.

The steps are rickety, and it smells like mold and rats. I cringe and force myself to stay strong as reality begins sinking in. We reach the bottom, and a lightly dimmed space comes into view. I can see three cells, all with bars. My body begins to seize with panic when I get a glimpse of their size. They're tiny, with no beds, no toilets, nothing. They're just cramped little spaces. I shake my head and dig my heels in. Blondie pushes me from behind, but I tighten my legs and refuse to move. He gives me a hard shove and I go soaring forward.

"Please," I beg, gripping the bars when he tries to shove me in. "Please don't make me go in there. I've done nothing wrong."

"Get in," he grunts.

"Are you human at all?" I scream.

He makes another grunting sound, swings the bars open, and throws me in so hard I slam against the back wall and collapse onto the floor. I charge forward, and he takes hold of me, uncuffing me quickly before slamming the bars in my face. I scream and wrap my fingers around them, shaking, screaming, and crying. Blondie just walks out, as if my crying doesn't affect him at all. I drop to my knees, sobbing. How did I end up here?

I hear a croaking sound and spin in my cell, my entire chest rising and falling with panic. Then I see Eric in the next cell, curled up and bleeding. "Eric?" I cry, crawling over and trying to reach through the bars between us. Eric chokes, and his body shudders.

"Eric!" I cry. "Wake up!"

He coughs and his eyes flutter open. "I . . . I . . . Indi?" he croaks.

"I'm here. Are you okay? Oh, Eric, I'm so sorry."

He coughs again, and groans in pain. I hear the sound of boots, and turn to see Blondie coming back with a small bottle of water. He shoves it through the bars, glares at me, and then turns and walks back up. He gave me water? Why? I crawl toward the bottle, my throat burning with desperation. I want to open it and devour it. Then I hear Eric coughing beside me, and I know this has to go between us both. I unscrew the bottle and press it to my lips.

The water is cool and soothing. Desperation wracks my body. It takes everything inside me not to drink the entire thing. My hands shake after a few deep pulls. I don't want to stop drinking, but I don't have a choice. My friend will die without this water.

I crawl toward the bars, and I gently push the bottle through. Eric is sitting up, his head hanging, his clothes torn and bloody.

"Hey," I whisper. "Here."

He lifts his head, and my heart twists when I see his blackening eye, his split lip, and the dried blood on his chin. He spots the water, and his eyes flare with need. He pulls himself toward me and snatches the bottle from my hands, tearing the lid off and pressing it to his lips. He drinks the water down in three large gulps. When it's empty, he lifts his eyes to me, looking like he feels even worse now.

"So thirsty," he croaks.

"I know," I soothe. "I will find a way to get us out of here, Eric. I swear."

"E . . . e . . . everything hurts," he whispers.

Tears sting my eyes. "I know, honey. I know. I'm going to find a way out of here, I promise."

"They're . . ." He takes a rasping breath. "They're going to sell you, Indi."

My heart hammers, and I swallow, trying to keep my face calm. "I know, but I won't let them. I *will* figure this out."

"We're on the ocean," he croaks. "How do we escape?"

"You listen to me," I whisper, reaching through the bars and touching his hand. "There is always a way."

"Indi . . ."

"No, Eric, don't you give up now. If you give up, we have nothing."

"I'm so hungry," he says, his eyes wide and pained.

"I know. Me too."

I lean back against the bars, still holding his hand. I hear his breathing become deep again, and I know his body is exhausted. He's been beaten, he's dehydrated, and he's hungry. If they don't feed us soon, the outlook isn't going to be good. I close my eyes, and they burn angrily. I focus on my breathing, and try to steady my pounding heart. I need to keep calm. I need to be strong and find a way to survive this.

If I don't . . .

Eric and I will both die.

I won't have that.

CHAPTER THREE

*Life is pretty good, and why wouldn't it be?
I'm a pirate, after all!*

Throwing up when there is nothing left in your stomach is the worst feeling in the world. I get seasick the next afternoon, and even though I'm dehydrated and starved, I end up crouched over throwing up bile because it's all I have left. Eric has passed out again, and he's looking worse and worse with every passing hour. I'm worried about him. He's not strong mentally, and he's been beaten, to add to the rest of the trauma we're experiencing. I think he's shutting down.

The pirates came in and gave us some food and water this morning. I gave mine to Eric. He didn't hesitate as he scarfed down my food, and then threw it all back up again. I knew that would happen. I warned him to eat slowly, but he didn't. I kept the water, slowly sipping it, gently easing my stomach into it. It didn't last long, though. Outside, the wind is howling and the ship is rocking. There is only so much my stomach can take.

I find myself the cleanest spot on the floor and curl up, as my stomach turns and protests. I close my eyes; my body is exhausted.

I know I need to turn my mind off and rest, but I'm terrified. How will we get off this ship? God, *will* we get off this ship? What happens after they sell me? Will they kill Eric? Dump him in the ocean? I would never sleep again knowing something had happened to him because of me. And, let's face it, this one is on me. I was the one who tried to run.

I feel my mind spin and I try to count, in a poor attempt to settle it. I need to rest. I need my strength. Everything inside me hurts, and the outside is so battered I don't even want to think about it. I just want to go home. I want to go and re-make every stupid decision in my life that led me to this point. Will I ever see another person again? Or will these pirates be all I know forever? Worse, if they truly do sell me, will I spend the rest of my life as a sex slave?

I shiver and my stomach coils tightly.

I won't cry.

They don't deserve that.

"Police!" someone suddenly yells.

Police? Like . . . sea police? I sit bolt upright, and my body screams in protest. I tilt my head to the side and try and listen to the noises above. Beside me, Eric begins stirring.

"Get the guns ready," another bellows.

"They're close, but they know they can't bring us in," a pirate barks. "Let them try. We will blow them to smithereens before they get the chance."

There are police close by? I get to my hands and knees, and my stomach turns angrily. Is this our chance for freedom? Can we escape? Eric is awake now, and he's staring at me, his gaze a little far off. "W . . . w . . . what's happening?"

"The police!" I cry. "They're outside."

His eyes widen, and he gets on his hands and knees too. "We need to make noise, scream for help."

"They'll kill us," I cry, shaking my head.

"They're going to kill us anyway, Indigo. Scream!"

"HELP!" I scream, my entire body filling with adrenaline. "Someone HELP!"

"HELP US!" Eric bellows loudly. "HELP!"

We hear cursing and shuffling on board, as well as loud yelling. Every inch of my skin tingles, and my heart is thumping so hard it is making me feel a little ill. This is it, possibly the only chance we'll ever get to escape.

"HELP!" We both yell at the same time, so loudly I have no doubt they've heard. We keep going.

I hear the cell door swing open, and Hendrix comes storming down. Okay, he is the last person I expected to see. His eyes are wild, and he charges in until he hits the bars. He grips them and glares at me. "Shut up," he barks.

"Like hell," I croak. "HELP!"

He pulls his gun from his jeans, and he points it at me. "Shut it, or I kill you."

"Do you think I care?" I scream. "Go ahead and kill me. It's got to be better than what you have planned."

Something flashes across his expression for a moment, before he turns his gun to Eric. My body freezes.

"But you do care if I kill him."

"Don't," I rasp.

He turns his dark gaze to me. "Shut your mouth. One more word and I fucking blow him to pieces in front of you."

"Just let us go," I cry.

"Didn't you hear me?" he bellows. "I said shut up!"

I get up to my feet, and everything inside me shakes. I walk over, gripping the bars and glaring through them. "Kill us then, you'll be doing us both a favor. HELP!"

He snarls, rips a key out of his pocket, and unlocks the bar. As soon as he pulls the door open, I charge. His arm lashes out and hits me in the chest, sending me flying backward. I land on my backside, but my body is full of far more determination than anything else he could throw at me. I lunge to my hands and knees, and I crawl forward, hitting his legs so hard he goes stumbling backward.

"Fuck!" he curses.

I crawl past him, and hit the bottom of the stairs before he grips my ankle, pulling me backward. I scream out loudly, and I feel him drop to his knees as he wraps his arms around my chest, pulling me backward. One large arm holds me to him while the other presses against my mouth so hard I feel my teeth bite into my lip. I squirm and kick, giving every ounce of fight I have inside. He slams my head back into his shoulder, and his hand tightens over my mouth.

"Stop," he orders.

I shove my head forward, and slam it back so hard he makes a loud *oomph*ing sound. He snarls and lets go of my mouth, pulling his gun from the floor and pressing it against my temple. "Don't make me kill you, because I don't fucking want to."

He doesn't want to?

He doesn't . . . want to?

I begin to shake violently, and I lose all my fight. My body slumps, and his arm flexes as he holds me up. He's panting, and my entire body moves with each angry breath he takes. He slowly lowers the gun from my head before pulling me back and getting to his feet, lifting me with him. He doesn't let me go; he simply takes me into the cell and lowers me down onto the floor. Then, finally, he lets go.

"Don't make this harder than it needs to be," he says. "I don't want to kill you or your friend, so just stay quiet."

I nod, and drop my head. He watches me a moment longer, before turning and storming out. I crumple backward, and a loud, wracking sob escapes me. There's no way out. We can't escape.

Eric crawls to the bars, and he gently whispers, "Indi, it's going to be okay."

"It's not okay," I wail, clenching my fists, and shaking my head from side to side. "Eric, he's going to sell me. What am I going to do?"

I lift my head to see Eric's face fall. "We're going to get out of this, I swear it, Indi."

"There is no way out!" I scream.

"I won't let anyone hurt you," he murmurs, reaching out and taking my hand. "I swear."

What he doesn't understand, in his goddamned black and white world, is that there's nothing he can do to stop any of this.

∼

They leave us in that cell for another entire night, and all of the following day. They didn't give us any more food or water. I have never wanted to die so much in my entire life. The idea of dying is so much kinder to my mind than the idea of living and slowly dehydrating, and suffering until my body can't take it anymore and shuts down. My tongue feels like it's a thick chunk of sandpaper. My throat is so dry I am terrified to swallow, because the pain is too much. My body has gone beyond starving, and is now verging on shutting down.

"Indi?" Eric croaks from his spot by the bars.

"I'm here," I whisper. My head is hanging, because it's too hard to lift.

"Are you okay?"

"I'm . . . getting there."

"We can't do this much longer. We're going to die if we don't do something soon."

"They won't let me die," I say, hoping I'm right. "I'm the prize money."

"Maybe they have found something else. We can't rely on that," he says, his voice so hoarse it's barely recognizable.

"What do we do, Eric?" I cry, trembling. I find myself having to stop and take a breath. "Because I sure as shit can't figure out how to escape this godforsaken ship!"

"We need a plan, for when they come back down," his voice is shaking and I'm sure his heart is pounding as hard as mine. "We can't see anything down here. We can't see rooms, or escape routes—nothing. We need a way to get up there."

He's right. Of course he's right. I know there's only one way out, and that's perhaps stealing a lifeboat, or a raft—or, hell, a barrel. There has to be something we can escape on, and getting up on deck to see is the only way to know. But how does one get up there?

"We're in a tiny cell, Eric. How do you suppose we get out? There are no windows."

"If you're their prize," he says, his voice low, "they won't want you to die."

"What are you getting at?" I whisper impatiently.

"I think you should pretend to have passed out when they come back down. They might freak, and take you above deck. You can scope the place out, find a way to escape."

"It's not a bad idea," I say, nodding. "But they might not come down here for days."

"Maybe not, but if they want you alive, they will."

I close my eyes, focusing on my breathing. "We can only try. There's no other option for us."

I hope this works.

We have nothing else.

CHAPTER FOUR

"I'm yer cap'n, and yer me lassie. For real, that be!"

"Indi," Eric whispers frantically. "Wake up!"

I stir from my spot on the floor and my entire body aches. I blink rapidly to try and focus my gaze on Eric.

"They're coming down!"

I try to move my body, but it really is stiff and sore. I hear the thumping above deck, and the sound of the cell door being unlocked. He's right; they're coming down. How many days has it been? I don't know.

"Pass out, Indi," Eric whispers. "Don't get up."

I stay in my position, trying to relax myself so that it looks real. I have to steady my breathing to make my body look less stiff. I hear the sounds of boots, and then the room seems to brighten. I can tell this, even though my eyes are closed.

"Please," I hear Eric beg. "She won't wake up. Please help her."

"Fuck, I told you to give her water," Hendrix barks to what I'm assuming is the pirate with him.

"I did, Cap," the pirate, murmurs back.

"I meant enough to fuckin' make sure she didn't end up like this. Did you fuckers even give them anything the past few days, like I instructed?" he bellows.

Silence fills the room.

Hendrix wanted them to feed us? He wasn't trying to kill us slowly. My chest swells with hope.

"Sorry, Cap, I thought . . . I thought Jess gave it to them and . . ."

"Fuck, incompetent idiots!"

I hear the cell door open, and a moment later I feel arms go around my body and lift me. I keep myself as floppy as I possibly can.

"Get Senny and Jess. They need to see to her."

There are women on the ship? My heart flutters. Women could mean hope. They might help me.

Hendrix carries me out, and I hear him order the pirate closest to him to get Eric water and food, and I'm thankful for that. More than anything, I want to make sure he's okay. When we get up and out into the halls, I crack my eyes open, frantically trying to take in my surroundings. Some doors are open, and in one room I can see a window. A window is good. I see inside the dining room, with its long tables and chairs scattered about everywhere. We pass a small kitchen; knives . . . knives could be good.

"I know what you're doin'," Hendrix suddenly says.

I quickly peer up at him to see he's looking down at me. Shit. He busted me scoping out his ship. He busted me pretending to be passed out. God, I am so stupid. I didn't even fool him for a minute, not even a damned minute. How am I supposed to escape when I can't even make him believe I've passed out for five minutes?

"Can't blame me for trying," I croak.

"What were you plannin' on doin'?" He smirks. "Overpowering me with your impressive strength, then running off with a knife and jumping overboard?"

Okay, well, now that he puts it like that I feel stupid. I frown and turn my eyes away from his.

"It wouldn't have worked for more than one reason, the main one being that we are in the middle of the ocean, a long way away from anything civil. You'd be dead in a day."

Asshole.

"I could have gotten overboard. It has to be better than just sitting here and waiting for you to sell me as some sort of sex slave," I snap.

He suddenly drops me to my feet. My knees buckle and it's only because of his tight grip around my arm that I don't crumple to the floor. I'm so weak. He begins to drag me, his pace angry and determined. He leads me down the hall and up the stairs onto the deck.

It's late afternoon, and the sun is just beginning to lower on the horizon. I squint, even though the sun isn't high in the sky. I've been in a dark cell for days, and it burns. He pulls me toward the railing and shoves me against it, pressing a hand to the back of my neck and pushing my face over the side.

What the hell?

"W . . . w . . . what are you doing?" I cry, struggling as much as my weak body will allow.

"Watch," he snarls, and then he turns his head. "Drake, get out here and throw some bait over!"

A minute passes, and then a chunk of thick meat is flung over the side of the ship. It lands in the water, making a small splash. Hendrix keeps his grip on the back of my head, and my chest begins to constrict. Then I see them. My vision blurs a moment, and my bottom lip trembles. At least six sharks, big ones, come up to the surface. One of them launches out of the water, snapping up the piece of meat as if it was no more than a bite-sized snack. I begin to cry. My entire body shakes, and panic fills me. Even if I find a way off, those sharks are deadly. I'd likely never get far. At least not in one piece.

"Do you see that?" Hendrix barks. "Do you fucking see it? That's what is in these waters. That's what happens if you try and leap over the side."

"I . . . I . . . I get it," I cry.

He shoves my head down farther, and I scream. "You want to be shark bait?"

"No," I scream, squirming.

"You want them to tear you to pieces, slowly?"

"Goddammit, no!"

He hurls me back up, and my body slams into his chest. My knees do buckle now, and he lets me fall. I hit the deck. My hands splay out on the damp wood, and I begin to pant. I'm done for. I have no way out. How do you escape something like this?

"My suggestion to you is to stop trying. There is no way off this ship, girl. Not without causing your own death."

I shake, my eyes darting around the ship. Looking for what? I don't know. That's when I see a tiny boat strung up at the back of the ship. I'm assuming they use it to get onto islands if they can't get the ship close enough. My heart pounds. I have two options here. I can take that small ship and run, or I can wait until Hendrix does the deal on land and take that small window to get away. Two options are better than one. Both could mean the end of my life. I'm willing to risk either.

Hendrix might have scared me, but I'm not about to give up.

Not yet.

∽

Hendrix lets me sit on the deck for a moment after the shark incident while he speaks to a group of pirates in the corner. He's deep in conversation, so I decide to take the risk. He is so sure he's scared me enough that I won't try and figure something out. My mind goes to the knives in the kitchen—hell, there's probably even a gun or two lying around. A shock attack, and I'd have to be careful, but I might be able to get Eric and get into the small boat at the back of the ship. I stand slowly, and very carefully I tiptoe toward the door that leads down to the second level.

I hold my breath as I take each step, so sure I will have a gun pressed to my head before I make it down to the last step. I get to the bottom, and slowly turn. He hasn't noticed. I pick up speed now, moving as quickly as I can down the halls. I get to the first room and run into it. I don't pay much attention to the bland wooden walls in the tiny room, or the single bed in the corner that looks like it's seen better days. I go straight to the drawers beside it and open them. Come on, there has to be a gun in here somewhere. Not finding one in this room, I run down to the kitchen. I hear voices, and know it's out of bounds. My heart begins to thump desperately. I have minutes, if I'm lucky. My eyes dart around, and I run to the next room that's open.

I go straight past the single beds—this one has two—and to the drawers. I yank them open and I begin shuffling through desperately. Come on. *Come on*. When I find nothing, I stand straight and spin around, only to come crashing into a flabby, big chest. My entire body stiffens, and I lift my face to see an old disgusting pirate, grinning down at me. He's got thinning gray hair, yellow teeth, and eyes that are a steely blue. He's awful. My blood runs cold. He's not giving me an expression that says he wants to hurt me. No, his expression is that of lust.

"Well, well, I heard there was a pretty girl on the ship. What're you doin' rummaging through my stuff, poppet?"

I shake my head, stepping back. "I was . . . I was just . . ."

"You know how long it's been since I've had a woman?" He grins, showing me rotting teeth.

Oh no.

What was I thinking, trying to run through this ship alone? I take another step back, but he lashes out and grips me. I try to squirm and fight, but my body is so weak. He spins me around, crushing an arm across my chest. Then he presses a knife to my throat. Oh no, please, God, no. Don't let this happen. *No.*

"Don't scream, or I'll slit it," he hisses into my ear.

Then his hands lower down over my stomach to my shorts. Everything in my world stops, and my entire body is stiff with fear. I can't move, even though everything inside me is screaming to fight. His hand slips into my shorts, and tears burn my eyes as his knife presses against my throat. I make a choking sound, and I plead with him to stop.

"Silence," he orders.

I feel bile rise in my throat as the tips of his fingers skim my panties. My vision begins to blur, and I struggle to find my fight.

When his fingers pull at the elastic of my panties, I find that fight. I drive my elbow backward suddenly, hitting him in the ribs. He bellows and stumbles backward, crashing into the drawers beside the bed. The knife drops to the floor, and I lunge for it. I wrap my fingers around it, and just as he goes to charge me I drop low, driving it into his leg. He screams, dropping to the floor. Blood runs from his leg, and the knife tumbles from my grip. I feel the blood drain from my face as I stumble backward. I've just . . . just . . . stabbed him.

I make a rasping sound, and I hear voices down the hall. I have to get out of here. I can't do this anymore. I drop to my knees, and the pirate is still rolling and screaming, gripping his leg. I grasp at the gun in his pants, and I pull it free. I push to my feet, and my hands wobble. I point the gun at him, and in a wobbly hiss, I snarl,

"Don't move." He is still groaning in pain, and I figure he hasn't acknowledged what I said. Blood is pouring from the deep wound in his leg.

"What the fuck?"

I hear Hendrix's angry voice, and spin to see him standing at the door, gun out.

"What are you doin'?"

"He tried to . . . he . . . he put his hands . . ."

"What did he do?" he says, his voice hard.

"He tried to rape me," I whisper.

Hendrix's fiery gaze turns to the pirate on the ground. "Is that a fact?"

"No boss, it's not . . . she's lyin'. She came in here and threw herself at me . . ."

Hendrix's face turns stony, and he pulls the trigger on his gun without a second question. I scream as a bullet enters right between the pirate's eyes. A clean hole appears, and blood begins to flow steadily from the wound. My entire body sways, and I can hear myself crying. I can't do this. I don't want to do this. I just want to leave. Why won't he let me leave? I'm tired. Exhausted. I'm done.

I lift the gun, and I press it to my temple. Hendrix turns, his eyes widen, and he very gently says, "Put that down, girl."

"What's the point?" I whisper. "My life is over anyway."

"It isn't what you want to do . . ."

"Isn't it?" I scream, my hand shaking. "What is it you think I want? To live my life as a sex slave? This is the better way."

Hendrix slowly raises his gun, only to about my thigh height. "Put it down, I don't want to hurt you."

"N . . . n . . . no."

I hear a shot fire out, I feel the burning in my thigh, and I feel myself collapse onto the floor. The gun falls from my hand and skids across the wood. I open my mouth, and nothing except a strangled gurgle comes out. I feel like there is fire spreading up my leg. It burns. I scream, and my hands instantly go to the wound where I feel hot, sticky blood.

Hendrix is there quickly, leaning down, and lifting me into his arms. "It's only a graze; you're okay."

"You shot me!" I bellow, my stomach twisting from the pain.

"I couldn't let you kill yourself. It isn't the right way."

"What would you know about the right way?" I cry.

"More than you think."

I tremble violently as he carries me down the halls. Everything is spinning, nothing makes sense. Everything in my world has been turned upside down, and I don't know how to deal with it. I feel sick with fear at the idea that I considered, even for a second, taking my own life. What about Eric? How could I do that to him? How could I be so selfish?

Hendrix takes me to his room, and he lowers me onto the sofa. He grips a phone from his desk, and he dials a number. I hear him bark something down the line, and then he's back at my side. He kneels down, gripping my shorts and tearing them clean off. I scream and squirm, but he doesn't stop. He lifts a shirt from the ground, and presses it to my leg. The pressure hurts, and I find myself pleading with him to stop.

"I'm saving your leg. Stop fighting me."

"You tried to kill me," I wail.

"I tried to stop you killing yourself. Now lie still," he orders, "or I'll make you lie still."

I sob and close my eyes, feeling tears flow down my cheeks. I feel sick inside; I've never been so terrified in my life. I'd take three rounds with Kane again over being in this situation.

"I only grazed you. A couple of stitches and you'll be fine."

"Why stop me?" I whisper, my voice having given up. "You don't care about my life. Surely you have other things to sell. Just let me have it my way."

"No," he says simply.

His fingers glide up my thigh, and for a split second, I forget the pain. He grips the top of my thigh, and turns me so he can get better pressure on my other leg. He doesn't move his hand when he stops moving me, and my entire body aches. The burning in my other thigh stops me from feeling too much, but I don't stop, not even for a second, feeling that hand on my thigh. Hendrix lifts his head, his eyes meet mine, and something passes between us. I don't know what it is . . . Maybe it's understanding? What could Hendrix possibly understand about me?

His finger begins moving in a gentle soothing circle, and he doesn't move his eyes from mine. My breath hitches, and I struggle to steady out my breathing. Hendrix's brown eyes scan my face, like he's looking for something he's sure he'll never find. He almost looks desperate. When his eyes fall back on mine, I feel his fingers squeeze my thigh . . . almost reassuringly. I don't understand him. I don't think I ever will.

"Cap?"

Hendrix jerks his hand off my thigh, almost guiltily, and then quickly stands up. He doesn't meet my gaze again, simply turns to the blond woman standing in the room. "Stitches. She needs about three."

She turns her gaze to me, and narrows her eyes. She's big, busty, and blonde. She's not ugly by any means, but she's not stunning either. With a growl, she walks in and over to the sofa. She kneels down, removing the tied shirt from my thigh and staring down at the wound. "Two should do it."

I close my eyes, feeling my stomach turning again.

I don't open them until she's finished and gone.

Then I turn to my side, and I close my eyes.

I don't want to see anyone.

∼

"You've earned yourself extra watch," Hendrix grunts later that night after I've woken up.

He stands in front of me, holding a towel. He thrusts it at me, and crosses his arms. Jackass. I slowly sit up, and my leg throbs. The blond girl used a locally injected painkiller, and I hope sterile equipment, but it's slowly starting to wear off and ache. I feel sick inside for resorting to pressing a gun to my temple. Would I have pulled the trigger? I really don't know, but for a moment, just a moment, I felt a weakness I've never felt in my life, and never plan on feeling again.

"If you think I'm going to try and escape after that experience, you're very wrong," I hiss, trying to control my body while it desperately attempts to expel the nothingness in my stomach.

"It doesn't mean I trust you. You will stay in here, with me. I will have someone lookout for you when I'm not in here. I don't trust you down in those cells, and I need to get you looking a bit healthier before I sell you to Chopper."

Chopper?

The name has my skin crawling.

"Please, reconsider . . ." I say, lifting my eyes to meet his. There has to be something inside him I can use to make him stop. I saw it for just a moment earlier, after he shot me. It was there . . .

He crosses his broad arms across his chest, and standing like that he looks incredibly handsome and powerful. God, he's dangerous; it's written all over him, from the way his muscles ripple and move when he does, to the way his clothes hug his hard, firm body.

His hair is loose this afternoon, and it hangs down to the base of his neck in thick waves. He has the kind of hair a woman would envy. The gold hoops in his ear glimmer. How can he be so beautiful, and yet so completely awful?

"All the pleading ain't goin' to change my mind. I have debts to pay. Don't take it personally."

"Don't take it personally," I snarl. "You're selling me to someone who is likely to use my body however he wants, but you don't want me to take it personally?"

He growls. "Listen, girl. I suggest you stop questioning my motives, and start learning to shut your mouth. I am not beyond hangin' you off the side of the ship again, further down this time, and lettin' the sharks have a go at catchin' you."

My eyes widen.

His tell me he's serious.

"I don't want to stay in here with you. Let me go back to the cell."

"Ain't gonna happen."

"I won't leave my friend. I will make your life a living hell if you keep me here—take it from me," I threaten.

"Is that a threat?" he growls, uncrossing his arms and stalking over to me.

"No, pirate. It's a promise. He's everything to me. I won't let you leave him down there to rot. Unless you're going to watch me every second of every day then you can't be sure I won't do whatever it takes to escape this. Including trying to take my own life again."

He takes a deep, ragged breath. "You would really do that to your friend? Kill yourself? Leave him alone on a ship to be killed?"

His words burn. "Sometimes, there is no choice."

"I will give you a choice," he says, meeting my stare dead on. "You either take it, or you don't. If you stay here, keep yourself safe, and don't attempt to run or hurt yourself again . . . I will continue to feed your friend. I will give him food and water, and when we stop I will let him go."

My eyes widen. He's offering Eric's freedom in return for me promising to stay and do as he asks. Basically, it's my friend's life or my own. If I say no, Eric dies. If I say yes, I am selling myself. I close my eyes. I already know the answer. I knew it from the moment I decided I would do whatever I could for Eric. I knew it when I decided moments ago that I wasn't going to show weakness. I had to be the stronger one. Eric will never know how close I got to giving up on both of us. I open my eyes and I meet Hendrix's gaze. "How do I know you're not lying?"

"Pirates' code. We make the deal in blood. I don't break my deals."

"You will swear that he will be fed and given water, and released with no strings attached? He can go back to his life and live it happily if I promise to do as you ask?"

Hendrix nods.

I close my eyes and hang my head. "It's a deal."

He steps forward, and I lift my eyes to see him bring out a knife. He slices it across his palm lightly. A small trickle of blood appears. I cringe, and my entire body begins to throb. I'm about to sign my life away. It's the only choice. At least with this choice I know Eric goes free. I can find a way to escape after. I'm sure I can. Hendrix reaches down and takes my hand, bringing the knife to my palm. I try to tug it away.

"No, I don't want to blend blood," I cry.

"Everything is sealed in blood—pirates' code. You don't seal it, I don't promise your friend's safety. I don't have diseases, so stop your crazy and shake my fuckin' hand."

He makes a line so fine on my palm I barely feel it. Only a tiny drizzle of blood appears. He reaches his hand out. I hesitate.

"How much is your friend's life worth to you? If you don't shake my hand, I don't make the deal. By blood, or by nothing."

"I don't break my promises. You hesitate a moment longer, and I will change my mind. If I change it, you won't get this chance again. Save your friend."

I stretch out my hand. If I die from a disease, so be it. My outcome really isn't looking too positive anyway. Hendrix reaches his hand out, and just before I touch it, he speaks the words. The words that bind me to him—at least, for now.

"By the code of the ocean, we make this deal."

I swallow, and I put my hand in his. One of his large hands covers mine, and I find myself shivering at the contact.

"By the code of the ocean," I whisper, "we make this deal."

He squeezes my hand, and then drops it. I quickly wipe my palm against my shorts and lift my eyes to his.

"It's done. You break my deal, I kill your friend."

I nod and lift my hand, inspecting the wound on my palm.

"You're not bleeding enough, which means you're dehydrated."

No shit, Sherlock.

"I will have Jess bring you food, water, and some clothes. You can shower, and you will be fed daily. I can't deliver you looking like a bag of bones."

God, did I look that bad?

"Fine." I nod.

"You can sleep on the sofa, and you have access to this room and the entire ship. Now you have made that deal, I will remove the watch. You even try to escape, I slit your friend's throat without hesitation. You can't get him out of those cells, so any notion of escape you might have . . . wipe it. I can see he means a lot to you, so it's your decision to keep him alive. You try and run, believe me, I will make it hurt for him."

"I get it, okay? I'm not fucking going anywhere," I snarl.

He narrows his eyes at me, and then he turns and stalks over to his desk. He picks up a phone and presses a few buttons.

"Jess, get me food, water, and some clothes for the girl. Bring them now."

He hangs up before the girl even gets the chance to answer. Five minutes later, a knock sounds out at the door. I turn on the sofa and watch as Hendrix goes over and opens the door, revealing something I didn't expect to see. There's a girl, I assume in her late twenties, standing at the door. I figured he had skanks on the ship, but this girl looks tidy, clean, and almost friendly. She has long, thick red hair and big green eyes. Her skin is pale, and her body is tiny and petite. What the hell is she doing on a pirate ship?

"Thanks," Hendrix says, taking the items from her hand.

She turns her eyes to me, and for a moment we hold each other's gaze. Could this girl be my way out? She gives me a small weak smile and then turns and leaves. Just how many women are on this ship? I thought it was some sort of rule that women didn't stay on pirate ships, but then, I didn't think pirates even existed in the world anymore.

I guess everything I believed in was wrong.

Hendrix walks over, dropping the things on the table in front of me. I see a tank top, a pair of jeans, a bottle of water, and a sandwich. My stomach twists angrily, and I'm not sure eating is a wise idea.

"Is that girl a prisoner too?" I suddenly ask.

Hendrix was just turning away, but at my words he stops and glares down at me. "She is here willingly."

"Why?" I blurt.

Why would anyone, in their right mind, stay on a pirate ship?

"Her life ain't your business. Nor are any of my crew's lives."

I narrow my eyes, but I drop it. I turn and stare at the sandwich again.

"I suggest you eat that, drink the water, get in the shower, and then rest."

"Like you care," I murmur, reaching over and gripping the sandwich.

"I have to give something worth wanting," he snaps. "Right now you wouldn't sell for even the cheapest price."

Ouch.

I don't answer him. I just lift the sandwich to my mouth and take a bite. The minute the food hits my tongue, I cringe. I'm starving, don't get me wrong, but my stomach has been starved for so many days that the idea of food and the reaction to food has it coiling angrily. I chew slowly, closing my eyes and focusing on my breathing. I have to eat, for my health and my strength. I swallow the chewed piece down, and wince at the pain in my throat.

"Don't go eating that too fast," Hendrix says. "You will only chuck it back up. Take it from me."

I glare at him. "What would you know? Have you ever been so starved the thought of food actually repulses you?"

He meets my gaze, his eyes deadly serious. "Yeah, I have."

He has? I blink. That wasn't the answer I expected. Unable to say anything to that, I turn my head back to the sandwich, and take another bite. It's ham and cheese, basic, simple, and if I wasn't feeling so ill, probably very yummy. I reach over and take the water bottle, unscrewing the top and bringing it to my lips. The desperation grips me again, and I want so badly to just swallow it all down. I know I can't. I have to go easy, so I take a few big sips and put it down. Then I take another bite of the sandwich, then stand and lift the clothes into my arms. I turn and walk off toward the bathroom without another look at Hendrix. I can't eat another bite until I have all this blood off me. I just can't.

The bathroom is actually quite large with a shower over a tub, a toilet, and a big square sink. I walk over, running my fingers over the razors and aftershave on the countertop. It's like being in a normal man's bathroom, only Hendrix isn't a normal man. I turn toward the mirror, and gasp when I see myself. Oh . . . my . . . God. He's right. I look hideous. My face is covered in peeling skin, my hair is ratty and disgusting, and my eyes are bloodshot and saggy and have dark rings under them. I'm usually quite tanned, with dark blond hair and big brown eyes. I actually like my looks. Right now, though, I look like a peeling snake.

I spin around and reach in to turn the shower on. The thought of soothing warm water has my body tingling in anticipation. I haven't showered for days. I remove my clothes, wincing as the fabric touches my raw burned body. I step into the shower, and the moment the water touches my skin I cry out. I grit my teeth, knowing I have no choice but to stay and endure this. I need it. My body needs it. I close my eyes, and steady myself by pressing my palms against the shower wall. The ship rocks slightly, and I widen my stance to stop myself from tipping over.

It takes about five minutes for my skin to feel better. When the pain eases, I lean down and fill my palm full of soap. I gently wipe it over the least burned parts of my body, and then I lather it into my hair. I find a washcloth, and I begin gently wiping my face, removing all the dead dried-up skin. I rinse my hair, my body, and my face, and then step out. I must admit I do feel fresher. My thoughts go to Eric. I should have requested that he get a shower. Maybe I can add it in. I dry myself gently, and then pull on the jeans and tank. They're a little big, but that's okay. They're clean and they're comfy.

When I'm done, I lift a comb from the counter and I run it through my hair. It takes me a solid fifteen minutes to detangle my blond locks, but when I look in the mirror again I can see a glimpse of myself. My face looks red, but far less hideous. Taking a deep breath, I turn and head back out. When I step out of the bathroom, I hear a giggle and turn my eyes to the far end of the room where Hendrix's bed sits. The blond girl who gave me the stitches is sitting on the edge of his bed, running her hands up and down his leg. Oh hell no, he's not seriously going to get it on while I'm in the room . . . is he?

I clear my throat.

He looks up, and his eyes widen. It takes a moment for him to put the serious expression back on his face. Was he shocked that I actually look like a female?

"Why is she in here?" she whines.

I wrinkle my nose, and mutter, "I'm his prisoner. Remember?"

"Is she going to be in here long?" She pouts, turning her gaze to Hendrix, who still has his eyes on me.

"She is," he murmurs.

"I don't recall having sex in front of me being part of our deal," I point out.

"I don't recall your opinion being part of it either." He smirks.

"I will make you wish you didn't stick her in front of me," I snap. "Believe me when I say I will make it impossible for you to get it up for her if you even attempt to fuck her in this room while I am in it."

He raises his brows. "Is that another threat?"

"No, again, it's a promise."

"Don't tell me fucking frightens you, *inocencia*?" he rasps.

What did he just call me? It sounded almost . . . Spanish.

I don't answer him. I simply turn and walk back to my sofa, dropping myself down and tucking my legs beneath me. I pick up the sandwich and water, and continue to nibble and sip. I hear the giggles behind me, then the distinct sound of sucking. He can't be serious? What sort of pig is he? I close my eyes, and I think of ways to piss him off enough to get him to stop. I know by now Hendrix isn't going to kill me: he loses too much if it does. So, I decide on the only thing I know I can do well.

I sing.

And I make it count.

"*Drink up me 'earties, yo ho, yo ho, yo ho! A pirate's life for me.*"

I repeat this over and over, at the top of my lungs. The girl growls after about five minutes, and I hear her stand and stomp her foot. "Make her shut up!"

I turn my eyes to Hendrix, and he's smirking at me. God, he's beautiful when he looks like that. I continue singing, not once moving my eyes from his. I raise my brows, as if to say, "Did you think I was joking?" He turns his eyes to the girl.

"Leave. I have business to take care of."

She huffs, and glares at me. "Next time, lock her up."

He gives her a bored expression, and she huffs once more before storming out. I turn my face back to the bottle of water in my hands, quite proud of myself. That'll teach him for trying to make my stay difficult.

"Proud of yourself, aren't you *inocencia*?" he says from behind me.

"Quite, thank you."

He snorts, and I look up to see him studying me, as if he's trying to understand me. *Good luck, buddy. I don't even understand me.* I meet his gaze, and I hold it. There's a challenge in his eyes, and I have no doubt he sees equal challenge in mine. I might have signed myself over to him, then to whomever he decides to sell me to, but damned if I'll stop fighting. Nothing will take away the spirit I have inside. If I have to drive him crazy, then so help his sorry ass, that's what I'll do.

"Where are you from, *inocencia*?"

Why does he insist on calling me that? What does it even mean?

"That's really none of your business," I throw at him, taking another bite of my sandwich.

"It is my business. You're my business now. So, answer the question."

"I'm originally from Australia."

He grins, wide. "I thought I detected an Australian accent. How long have you lived in the United States?"

I cross my arms, and then swallow the food in my mouth. "What is this? A checklist for the man you're selling me to? Trying to make sure I am up to standards? Well, don't bother, pirate. I'm not telling you anything. I might be following your rules but it doesn't mean I like you, or respect you. Get that through your head."

His entire body stiffens, and he storms forward, gripping my shoulder and hurling me up. As soon as I land on my feet, he brings his face down close to mine, and his voice comes out steely and rough. "Do not forget I am the one holding your friend in my cells. I can go down there, slit his throat, and then sell you anyway. I owe you nothing, girl. Don't push me."

"You made a deal," I whisper, feeling my rage building.

He lets me go, and I stumble backward onto the couch. He straightens and turns, taking lengthy, determined strides until he reaches the door. He spins around and glares at me. His fingers grip the doorframe. "Don't push what you don't know, *inocencia*. Even the strongest men and the strongest deals . . . can be broken."

Then he turns and leaves the room.

What the hell?

∼

I sit for only a few minutes before deciding that, if I'm allowed to start walking around the ship, then I will make good use of it. I step out of the room, and begin walking down the halls that lead to the cells. I want to talk with Eric, see if we can figure out a way to escape together. I can't leave him behind—if I do, he dies. If I go, it has to be with him, or I have to at least make sure he goes safely on his own.

I put my head down, and try to make it to the cells as quickly as I can, but midway there I run into the blond bimbo Hendrix had in his room. She reaches out as I try to duck past her, and her fingers curl around my upper arm. Then I'm being slammed against the wall. I close my eyes and grit my teeth. I won't be bullied by this beast. It won't happen. I take a deep breath and open my eyes to meet her angry glare.

"Listen to me, you little whore. Hendrix is mine. I don't care what deal you two have going: the next time I come into his room I am going to get what I need."

Ew.

"If you think I'm going to let you bully me into making the decision to stop cock-blocking Hendrix, you will find yourself at a dead end. I won't be bullied, and I sure as shit won't sit around and let him fuck your trashy brains out in front of me."

Her eyes flare, and she raises her fist. I see it coming, and I know how to block it. Call me a seasoned pro, but I've learned how to dodge punches. As soon as her fist flies forward, I twist my body from her grips, and swing my head to the side. Her fist hits the wooden wall, and she screams in pain as it splinters and her hand goes right through it. Before I can react any further, the tall, blond man who threw me in the cells originally—Drake, I think—is pulling me back.

"Enough," he barks.

"Oh God," the blond girl screams. "Drake, my hand is stuck in the wall."

"That will teach you for running your mouth off," he barks.

He's . . . defending me? I squirm in his grips, but he doesn't let me go.

"I said enough, girl. Stop squirming."

"Then let me go," I snap.

"No," he says simply, before reaching over, gripping the blond girl's shirt and pulling her so hard her hand comes out of the wall. It's got blood and splinters all over it.

"Go and see Jess, Senny, and get your hand sorted out."

Senny is the blond girl's name. She spins, gripping her hand and glaring at me. "This isn't over."

"It is over."

I hear the booming voice and turn to see Hendrix appear from the shadows of the hall. How long had he been standing there? He walks over to Senny, grips her shoulder, and leans in close. "You touch anyone on my ship again, male or female, I will slice you up and toss you overboard. You're no more than an easy fuck, Sienna. That's it. I don't owe you anything, so I suggest you shut your mouth and stay away from Indigo."

I feel my body tense. It's the first time I've heard him use my name.

Sienna/Senny nods frantically, and turns and rushes off. When she's gone, Hendrix turns to me. "Cock-blocking?"

I bite my lower lip and look away.

"Where'd you learn to dodge punches like that?" he adds.

I shrug, still staring at the floor. Drake is still holding onto me, saying nothing.

"I just reacted . . ."

"What did I say about lying?" he growls. "You will learn very quickly that I can tell a liar from a mile away, so don't bother trying. Now, I ask again, where did you learn to dodge punches like that?"

I'm sick of his arrogant attitude. He's always so pushy, so dominant, so frustrating. I wiggle from Drake's grip, and he steps back and lets me go. I cross my arms and face Hendrix, my eyes wild with adrenalin and rage. "I learned it because my ex-boyfriend used to beat me so much I had to defend myself. One night, I couldn't defend myself, so I shot him and he went to jail. Now he's free and looking for me. I had to learn to defend myself, otherwise he would have killed me. Does that answer your question?"

Hendrix's expression is hard to read, but his eyes are intense. They're focusing on me, and he looks like he's deep in thought. I shake my head, and turn to Drake. "Thank you, for whatever that was."

He focuses his blue eyes on me and I see a flash of something else inside them. He looks . . . lonely. He holds his life in his eyes, and from what I can see it's a life of bad painful things. The scar on his face tells me that. I hold his gaze, wondering about the man that is behind the giant. He's so big, so muscly, so powerful, yet his face . . . it holds a certain level of gentleness. He turns his eyes away from mine and nods, before turning and walking off.

"Don't make friends with Drake; he's not the kind of man you'll understand," Hendrix says.

I rip my eyes from Drake, and turn to Hendrix. "You said I could do whatever I wanted on this ship, so long as I took care of myself. That's what I'm doing."

I turn and begin walking toward the cells again.

"Is he still after you?" Hendrix yells out.

I stop, and my entire body stiffens. I look over my shoulder and murmur, "It doesn't matter, because it's none of your business."

He makes a growling sound as I disappear into the dark.

What does it matter to him anyway?

CHAPTER FIVE

Yo ho, haul together, hoist the colors high!

"You what?" Eric rasps, widening his eyes.

I wrap my fingers around the cell bars, and peer in at him. "It was the only way to keep you safe, Eric."

"You basically sold yourself to him," he yells.

"I had no choice."

"You knew he wouldn't have hurt you. You didn't have to make that deal."

"He might not have hurt me," I cry, "but he would have hurt you."

"Indi . . ."

"I'll get us out of this mess. I just need some time. For the moment, he thinks I am not going to do anything because I want to protect you. If I can get you out . . ."

"Even if you can, how do we escape?" he whispers, letting his eyes dart around the small space.

"If I can get the key we can sneak out really late at night when Hendrix is asleep. There's a lifeboat at the back of the ship. I might be able to start hiding some water in there . . . It might give us a few days . . ."

"As soon as he knows you're gone he will come looking. He will find us out there . . ."

"Do you just want me to give up?" I snap. "Lie down and let my life be sold?"

"No, but we need a more solid plan."

"We're in the middle of the ocean, Eric. There's nothing more solid than that."

"We can't just jump overboard, Indi. It doesn't work like that."

"Well when you figure out a better plan," I bark, "do share."

Then I spin around and storm toward the door.

"Indi!" Eric yells. "Don't start acting stupid."

Acting stupid?

Is he serious?

I am laying my freedom down for him, and he thinks I'm acting stupid.

I don't look back at him, nor do I stop. I walk up the stairs, slamming the door behind me, only to run smack bang into Jess. She squeaks and jumps backward, her big eyes wide. "I'm sorry, I didn't realize you were there."

I shake my head, putting my hands up. "It's fine. I'm fine."

"Are you okay?" she asks softly.

I feel my body relax a little, and I exhale a loud breath. "I'm fine, thank you."

"I'm Jess. We haven't been formally introduced."

She extends her hand to me, and I wearily take it. "I'm Indigo."

"That's a pretty name." She smiles.

I smile back. "Thank you. Is Hendrix around?"

"He will be in the dining room at this time of the day."

I smile again. "Thank you."

She nods, and then shrugs. "Anytime, that's what I'm here for."

I so desperately want to ask her why she's on this ship but I can't. If she's working closely with Hendrix then she is likely to tell him everything I say or do.

"Thank you," I say once more, before turning and heading up toward the deck.

I need fresh air.

I need to think.

When I reach the deck, I see a group of pirates near the navigation cabin. They are all smoking and talking amongst themselves. I don't meet any of their gazes as I walk past them to the edge of the old yet beautiful ship. I peer overboard, and see a sculpture of a mermaid soaring off the front. I smile, and I realize it's the first real smile I've given in days.

I can hear the faint chatter of the pirates behind me, and I zone out, forgetting where I am for just a moment. I close my eyes and let the sea breeze tickle my face. I take a deep breath and fill my lungs, enjoying the slight burn as they expand.

"Best not get too close to the edge." I hear a raspy voice behind me. "There's a lot of sharks down there, but I'm sure the cap'n has already told you that."

I spin around to see three pirates standing, staring over at me. They're all older, and they look kind of mean. One of them laughs at the nervous expression on my face, but the laugh isn't gentle or kind. It frightens me. I step back against the side, gripping on.

"Oh, now, don't be scared, lassie. We ain't gonna hurt ya."

Why don't I believe him?

"Just leave me alone . . ."

The pirate standing in the middle takes a step forward, and my entire body stiffens. "Just warnin' you about them there sharks. Why, if you fall overboard, you're toast."

"I know," I say, trying to keep my voice steady.

"You seen them, then?" He grins. "Well you wouldn't want to trip . . ."

He steps forward quickly, and I scurry backward, slipping and gripping onto the railings to stop myself falling over the side. All three of them roar with laughter, and my entire body tingles with fear. They're trying to bait me, trying to tease and taunt me. They would find it absolutely hilarious if I was to fall over the side right now. I feel my eyes burning, and I turn away, trying to steady my wobbling legs.

"Aw, now, don't go gettin' all upset. Why . . . we're only havin' fun."

Assholes.

"Yeah," one says. "We wouldn't want you to die on us now . . ."

"Leave her alone."

I hear the voice, and turn my head to see Drake standing behind the group of guys.

"Now, Drakey-boy, ain't no one doin' anything wrong."

"Leave. Her. Alone."

His voice is like razor blades, and the pirates grumble and snort before turning and walking off. My entire body slumps with relief. Thank God. Drake stares at me a moment before starting to turn away. I can't let him leave without a thank you; he just rescued me, yet again.

"You like saving me?" I say timidly.

He stops turning, and looks back at me. "Just doing my job."

"Your job is to save the captives?"

His lip twitches. Oh my, does Drake smile?

"It is my job to make sure you don't get hurt."

"So he can sell me in one fine piece? Right?"

He shrugs. "Something like that."

"So you don't do it because you're a nice person, then? That's a real shame," I say, finding an old bench and sitting on it. "Because I kind of liked you."

His eyes fall on me, and he looks confused, like he can't possibly believe I could like him or even contemplate liking him. Then he does something that surprises me: he walks over and sits down beside me. Compared to my small frame, he's massive. I still can't wrap my mind around the sheer size of him. We both stare out at the ocean for a moment, just sitting in silence, and then I turn to him.

"How come you're so big?" I ask.

He shrugs, and I can see the muscles in his arms move as he does. "I used to play a lot of football back in school, but I was always a big kid. I did some security work for a large bar chain in the United States for a while. That took a lot of work, because I had to be big to be able to throw the drunken idiots out. I worked out hard, and got bigger. Then I met Hendrix and joined the crew, becoming his main security man. I am always with him when he goes to shore, and I keep this ship in line when he can't."

"So you don't work out now?" I say, shocked.

He shakes his head. "Not all the time, but I do lift a lot."

"You're kind of . . . scary."

His lips twitch again. "That's kind of the point."

"I guess it is."

He turns his face, and looks down at me. "But you're not scared of me."

"No," I say, shaking my head. "I'm not."

"Why?"

I shrug. "I don't know. I guess I see something that maybe you don't."

"And that is?"

"Kindness."

He flinches, and turns his face away from mine, but not before I see a moment of pain in his eyes.

"You've been hurt really badly, haven't you?"

He stands suddenly. "I shouldn't be talking to you. Hendrix wouldn't agree."

"Hendrix doesn't own me," I protest.

He looks down at me once more, then reaches out, lifts my hand, and turns it over so he can see the faint red line from where Hendrix sliced me when we made our deal.

"But you're wrong," he says. "He does own you."

Then he drops my hand and walks off.

There's something very deep about Drake. He has a darkness and yet an equal amount of light. He's had a difficult time with life, of that I'm sure. Yet he seems to have found a way to find the goodness in people.

And I have a feeling he might be one of the only friends I'll make on this ship.

CHAPTER SIX

Work like a captain; play like a pirate.

The first few nights in Hendrix's room go reasonably well. He's not here very often, so I spend my evenings alone on the sofa, or down with Eric. I have been trying to make small talk with Hendrix, but most of the time I fail. I so desperately want to see if there's a chance of any kind of connection between us. It's a far-off dream, I do know this, but it's worth a try. If Hendrix likes me, even a little, he might reconsider selling me to repay his debt. That's what I'm hoping for, at least. It's got to be better than living in fear. I've figured out that my life is safe for the moment.

I'm making the most of that moment.

My dinner tonight is boring and simple, but it's food, and I'm not going to turn anything down. I eat as slowly as possible, trying to ease my stomach back into taking nourishment. The past few days have been all about experimentation with food and water. The bland mashed potatoes are heavy and filling, but they seem to sit well in my stomach. When I finish up my dinner, I have another shower and find myself a long, overly loose shirt in the small pile of clothes Jess gave me. I slide it on and find myself a comb before heading out to the sofa.

Hendrix is at his desk when I step out, and he looks up when he hears the door creak. His eyes are intense as pins them to mine. It's hard not to create something sexual when the air crackles every time he walks into the room. It's strong, and intense, and so alluring. I watch as he lets his eyes travel down my body, before lifting back up to my face. He looks like he's satisfied. "You're looking healthier. It's good."

I cross my arms and walk over to the sofa, sitting down and running the comb through my damp hair. "I don't feel all that much better."

"Has your leg healed?"

I shift uncomfortably, and stare down at the small purple scar on my leg where he shot me—well, where he grazed me. "It's fine," I mutter.

Hendrix is flicking through some papers on his desk, and I notice his eyes are narrowed like he's deep in thought. He opens a drawer and pulls out a phone. My eyes widen, and I try to smother the gasp that escapes my lips. Hendrix has a phone? Oh God. He lifts the tiny device up and punches in a number before bringing it to his ear. He waits a moment, not looking at me, probably not even thinking about the fact that he's just shown me a way out.

"JR, yeah, it's me. You got his location yet?"

I watch him nod.

"Fuck. Yeah. Let me know when you do."

He brings the phone down, and growls a curse. He's obviously having a bad night. He turns and storms toward the bathroom, muttering something about incompetent idiots. He slams the door, and I leap to my feet. I don't think, I don't hesitate, I just run toward the phone on the desk. I flip it open, darting my gaze to the bathroom door. Oh God, I have seconds, maybe minutes, if I'm lucky. He could walk back out at any moment.

Adrenaline fills my veins, and I begin to shake as I fumble with the keys, punching in Eric's mother's number. I know it by heart, because we've been close for so many years. My heart is thumping, and my head is spinning as I struggle to catch my breath. Come on. *Come on.* I have just brought the phone to my ear when a hand lashes out and thumps my wrist, sending the phone flying. I spin around, crying out, and lunge toward it, landing on my knees and wincing in pain.

Hendrix is on me in seconds, flattening his body over mine. He lashes out and grips my wrist as I attempt to reach out for the phone. His hard body is crushing me into the floor, but I still squirm, desperation taking over.

"Enough," he rasps into my ear, tightening his grip on my wrist. Tears burn my eyes, and I struggle to blink them back. *No weakness.* I swore I'd show no more.

"Just let me go. I don't want you to sell me!"

He flips me over and puts his hands on either side of my head, pinning me with his gaze. "You made a deal, a choice."

"You didn't give me many options," I yell, squirming.

"You're not in the position to be given options."

His dark eyes are piercing and deadly.

"Just get off me, get off me!" I cry, squirming.

"This is the only phone on the ship," he growls. "It will now remain with me at all times."

"You're a pig!" I spit as he moves his body from mine.

I scramble to my feet and turn, rushing toward the sofa. I drop down onto it, sinking into the old, well-used cushions. I grip the sheet, and I pull it up over my head before letting the tears escape my eyelids. I sob quietly, not wanting him to hear my weakness.

He doesn't leave the room, and he doesn't speak to me again, but I know he can hear me. I know he can hear my pained whimpers as I cry myself to sleep.

It's dark, and I can hear his soft breathing. A faint light is coming underneath the door, and it shines just enough for me to see his silhouette. I am on my hands and knees, crawling toward him as quietly as I possibly can. I know he's got the phone on him, and I know I'm going to give it one last shot. I can't give up that easily. I can't just lie down and accept my fate. I have to try, just once more.

I reach his bed, and I rise up onto my knees, staring down at him. Why does he have to look so beautiful? Why does the light have to caress his body, showing every stunning curve of muscle? I reach down and gently place my hand on his leg, slowly moving it up. He makes a grunting sound, and I freeze quickly. A moment later, he's breathing deeply again. I slide my hand up higher until I reach his pocket. Nothing in there. I reach over gently and try the other one. I feel a hard bump.

My heart begins to pound.

I flex my wrist, and then I gently angle it so that I can reach into his pocket. I can just feel the top of the phone when his hand moves at lightning speed and grips mine. He wraps his fingers around my wrist, and he tugs. I go soaring forward and land half over his body, with my legs dangling off his bed. I squirm, but his other arm comes up and pins my hips, pressing me down into him.

"You just don't give up, do you?" he murmurs.

It takes me a moment to respond, because I am completely dazed by the smell of him. His skin has a warm heat radiating off it, and the smell is a blend of rum and man. I swallow, and my vision swims as I realize how good it feels to be draped over him. I shake my head, horrified at myself for even taking a moment to enjoy the feeling of him against me. I tug my wrist free from his hand, and he snorts, tightening his arm over my hips.

"Did you really think I'd make it easy for you?" I snap.

"I did, considering you tied your friend's life to your behavior."

I freeze.

Eric.

I stopped for just a second, thinking about how this could impact him. I close my eyes, horrified with myself.

"Did you truly think you could sneak up on me and take that phone?" he says, his fingers flexing on my hips.

"Let me go."

"Answer me, *inocencia*."

"No, I did not, pirate. But I had to try. I might have put my life before my friend's, but it doesn't mean that I will just roll over and accept it when I see a window of opportunity."

"So stupid," he murmurs, and his fingers begin making circles on my hips. I stiffen.

"L . . . l . . . let me go."

"In good time."

What the hell?

"What makes you think you can just do whatever you want?" I whisper, tugging my body backward in another poor attempt to wriggle free.

"I'm a pirate. I make the rules on the ocean, and I break the rules on the ocean. I'm untouchable out here."

"It doesn't make you invincible, pirate. I'll make you pay for this. One day, I'll find a way to make this burn."

He chuckles softly. "I know you will, *inocencia*."

"And how do you know that?" I bark.

He lets me go, and my body slides down onto the floor.

"Because you're fire," he murmurs. "And fire never stops burning."

CHAPTER SEVEN

"There she blows!"

The first week passes with no more drama. I spend most of my time down with Eric, and we talk as much as we can about escape, though the longer I am here the less I think escape is actually an option until we stop on dry land—if we stop. I am grateful, however, that Eric is being fed and cared for. Hendrix has been living up to his end of the deal, so I have been living up to mine. I have been eating and taking care of myself, and I haven't tried to escape again.

Staying in Hendrix's room has been interesting, to say the least. He spends most of his time at the little desk in the corner on the phone that I can't have, barking orders at people and organizing things that, from the sounds of them, aren't things I wish to know about. Nighttime is the oddest. Trying to sleep when he's in the bed just over from me is . . . awkward. It's even worse when he gets up in the morning and walks right past me, half-naked with morning wood. I won't lie: the man has impressive morning wood.

I hate that I'm looking, and part of me has considered that I am temporarily insane, but it's hard to turn away. The man has a body that is unlike any I've ever seen. His chest is broad and defined, his abs trim and strong, and his skin is that beautiful bronze color. His chest has a range of tattoos, all of them gray and black; there is no color. His arms are both fully sleeved, but his back has nothing—nothing but gorgeous, olive skin over hard, defined muscle.

I won't lie and say that I don't open my eyes in the morning and watch him walk past. His hair is always sleep-mussed, and his eyes are always heavy, with those thick lashes on display for me to admire. I find myself clenching in the morning, hating that my body is acting against my better judgment, and tightening itself with want for a man I really don't like. It's wrong, but God help me, I can't stop looking. I don't even know if I want to stop looking.

On the eighth morning I wake before Hendrix, which isn't something that usually happens. I slide off my place on the sofa, and creep into the bathroom. I haven't showered for a few days because I've been spending all my time down with Eric. By the time I get back, I'm exhausted. I've spent the day trying to convince Eric that it's going to be okay, but he's taking it out of me. I usually fall onto the sofa when I get back, and don't move.

I need a shower today though. I am finally feeling more like myself, and my skin is beginning to heal nicely, so I figure it's time to go into the shower and remove the last of the dead skin that's left. This is the perfect time to do it.

I step into the bathroom, and close the door behind me. I drop the loose dress I am wearing, and I turn the water on. When it's warm enough, I step in. A content sigh leaves my lips, and I close my eyes, tilting my head back and letting the water run over my body and head. I reach my hand out until I find a bottle of shampoo, and I tip some into my hand before bringing it to my hair and lathering it through. Oh, that's nice.

I finish up with my hair and give my body a good scrub, removing the last of the dead skin that is left behind from the sunburn. When it's gone, I wash it once more and then step out. I go to take a towel, only to see there's none left. My eyes widen, and I curse. Shit, you have to be kidding me! No towel? I look down at the dress on the floor, only to see it's soaked from the water I splashed out. I have to go out and get the one off the sofa. I walk to the door, and crack it open. Hendrix is still asleep, his big arms tucked up behind his head and his chest rising and falling heavily.

I decide to make a run for it. I step out of the shower and begin rushing toward the sofa, but I don't make it. I trip and fall on a pillow that's been tossed onto the floor, and I land with a thump and a scream. The light is flicked on in a matter of seconds, and I am scurrying backward to try and get back to the shower. Before I can make it, Hendrix appears, sleep-roused and holding a gun toward me. I do the only thing I can think of: I throw my hands up.

His eyes widen, and his mouth drops open.

It's only then I realize what putting my hands up has done to my position.

I'm now on the ground naked, with my hands in the air.

"Holy fuck," Hendrix hisses.

I drop my arms and try to cover myself. If I move, he will see all I have to offer. I lift my legs, trying to hide myself. Hendrix grips the towel from the sofa and tosses it at me, not once taking his eyes from my body. Why does that have me breaking out with goose bumps?

"I . . . I . . . there wasn't one in the shower, and . . ."

"You have beautiful skin," he says, his eyes now focused on my shoulders.

"I . . . um . . ."

"It's like silk, so damned pretty. I didn't know you were so fuckin' perfect."

Oh God.

He stares at me for a minute at least, his eyes blazing with something I can't decipher, and then suddenly he shakes his head as if he can't believe what he's just said. Then he stiffens, and growls, "Chopper will love it" before turning and rushing out the door, slamming it loudly.

What the hell was that?

∼

Salty wind. It's my daily pleasure. I love to stand in it and breathe it in. I love the way it makes my hair curl and tangle. I love the way it makes my skin feel. This morning the wind is light and cool, and the ocean smells divine. I grip the side railings on the ship, and stare out. I haven't seen Hendrix since our little run-in earlier; he's managed to find a way to avoid me. I even went looking for him, but couldn't find him on the ship. I'd love to know how he did that.

I turn, staring over at the lifeboat. I still wonder about escaping on it. I don't know if I can, or what my chances are, but it's more than once crossed my mind. I peer around the deck and see that no one is up here, so I head over to it. I'm halfway up when I trip on a pile of ropes on the ground. I land with a thump and curse loudly. Dammit. I go to move, only to realize my leg is tangled in one of the thick ropes. I squirm and tug, twisting my foot, only to tangle myself more.

"What're you doin'?" I hear Hendrix's voice coming from behind me.

Of course he chooses now to come over.

"I got stuck."

He leans down, gripping my foot and trying to untangle it.

"How the hell did you get it so tangled?"

"I don't know," I mutter. "Trying to untangle it?"

He shakes his head and crouches down, twisting my foot to try and get it out. I squirm and pull, and he slaps my thigh. "Stop moving."

My mouth drops open. He stops moving, as if he realizes what he just did.

"Did you just . . . slap me?"

"If you quit moving, I wouldn't have had to."

My mouth hangs open.

"Close that, before I find a good use for it," he growls, lifting his dark eyes to meet mine. My skin tingles.

"Stand up. This will be easier if you do," he orders. He stands, taking me with him, and I lose my balance when I accidentally try to lift the wrong foot. Hendrix reaches out, taking my shoulder, and goes to take a step forward to steady me, only to realize he's wrapped the rope around his own ankle and is now tangled too. As if in slow motion, we topple backward. I scream, and land with a thump on the ground as the ropes surround me. Hendrix lands over me, but manages to put his hand down to stop me taking the force of his body. He's pressing into me in places he really shouldn't be.

"Fuck," he curses, tugging his hand to try and untangle it.

"How the hell did you get tangled too?" I cry out, squirming.

"Stop fuckin' squirming like that," he orders, and I stop as soon as I realize why he's asked me to. He's hard. My God, he's hard.

"You're . . . you're . . ."

"I'm fuckin' hard because you're squirming against me. I'm a man. Get over it."

I gape up at him, and he gives me a determined glare before tugging one of his hands and freeing it. He reaches down and untangles my hand, and I shift to try and move my feet.

"Stop fuckin' moving. You're tangling us again."

"Well, I can't just lie here and not move," I protest. "Why don't you just get up and let me figure myself out."

"If I leave it up to you, I'll come back next week to a bag of rotting bones."

"That's mean," I snap.

"Stop fucking squirming," he hisses.

I didn't realize I was squirming again. I try to stop myself, and I let him focus on untangling us. Stopping has me focusing on his erection pressing against my thigh, and that's really not a good thing. I close my eyes and try to focus on anything else but the way his body is flexing and moving against mine.

"It's very hard not to move when you're all over me," I mutter.

"Didn't intend on bein' all over you," he snaps back.

"Well, you are. Maybe *you* should stop moving."

"Why?" he taunts. "You likin' it?"

I turn my eyes away guiltily. "I don't . . . *dislike* it."

He jerks back and stares down at me. He's shocked; I can see it written all over his face. He never expected me to admit to something like that. Well, he was wrong. We stare at each other for such a long time my heart begins to pound uneasily. He wouldn't try to . . . kiss me? Would he? I bite my lower lip, trying to pull my eyes from his yet finding that I'm so completely captivated that they are refusing to move.

"Errr, Cap?"

We both turn our heads to see Drake staring down at us.

"Drake, cut these fuckin' ropes."

"Yes boss," he says, but I can hear the humor in his voice.

"It's not funny, Drake," I snap.

He doesn't answer; he just cuts us free. After Hendrix pulls himself to his feet he reaches down and pulls me up too. I kick the strands off my foot and refuse to meet his gaze as I hurry off.

"'Thank you' would be nice," Hendrix yells.

"Thank you," I cry, and scurry down the stairs.

God, could it get any worse?

CHAPTER EIGHT

Ahoy, me hearty!

I hide in shame for the remainder of the day. My cheeks flush every time I think about my little moment with Hendrix. I decide today I won't go and see Eric; I just need to think. When night falls, I go to bed early, trying to avoid any confrontation. I'm becoming bored and desperate, and the only thing I can do is sleep. Tonight, however, sleep isn't happening. I just can't settle, and my body is restless. I decide after much debate, to make a dash to the kitchen. I need milk. It fixes all my sleeping problems.

I climb off the sofa and sneak out to the kitchen. When I get inside, I flick on the light and tiptoe in until I reach the fridge. Opening it, I rifle through until I find a bottle of milk. I take it out, and pour some into a glass before popping it into the microwave. I hit 30 seconds and wait. The ship is noisy this evening. I guess the guys decided it was time to party. The microwave dings, and I pull my warm glass out, swishing it around before bringing it to my lips. The warm liquid soothes my dry throat, and I sigh.

I turn to head back out, when the kitchen door swings open and Hendrix comes stumbling in. Oh magic, he's drunk. He doesn't notice me at first, and walks over to the cupboard, opening it to pull out a packet of crackers. I clear my throat, and he spins, sending crackers flying across the floor. I snort a laugh, and wrap both of my hands around my milk to stop it from spilling.

"What the . . .?" he mutters.

His eyes are glassy, so my guess is that he's had more than just a few. I hold up the glass. "Just getting milk. You guys are noisy and I couldn't sleep."

He begins walking toward me, and the look on his face has my heart speeding up. "Could always join in, *inocencia*."

Why the hell does he keep calling me that?

"No thanks," I mutter, trying to step past him.

He puts his arm out, stopping me. "You scared of me?"

I tilt my head up and meet his eyes. "No, not at all."

"Then why won't you join in?"

"Because you don't really want me to, and because I'm only here because I made a deal with you to behave. You're selling me. There's really no point in me trying to befriend anyone."

"Keep your friends close," he murmurs, stepping closer, "and your enemies closer. Didn't anyone teach you that, *inocencia*?"

"They did," I whisper, biting my lower lip.

Why does he have to come so close? I can smell the rum on his breath as he leans down, meeting my gaze. God, he's gorgeous. Tonight he's wearing a tight black T-shirt, with a pair of faded blue jeans, heavy black boots, a dog chain around his neck and his dark hair is ruffled and messy. He has these thick gold and silver chains around his wrists that just seem to give him something extra. Perhaps that touch of bad boy that is needed for his look.

"There are many ways to get to sleep," he says, staring down at my lips.

Shit.

Walk away, Indigo.

"Sure there are," I try to say, but my voice wavers. "This is just the best one."

"A warm body usually does the trick for me, sweetheart."

Did he just call me *sweetheart*? Why is my heart thumping over that?

"I have a name, you know?"

A small, gorgeous grin spreads across his face. Lordy, he's beautiful when he smiles. "*Indigo,*" he purrs.

"I should . . . go."

I try to squeeze past him, but his hand lashes out and grips my hip. I stiffen and swallow, turning toward him. He takes another step closer, and stares down at me. "If I didn't have to," he murmurs, "I wouldn't sell you. You're just what I need."

I stiffen and shove him back. "You're such a jerk. I'm no one's bedmate!"

His eyes widen, and he takes a step back. "And yet you're the one who is wet at the thought of me."

"Don't flatter yourself," I snarl.

"If I put my fingers between your legs right now, *inocencia*, you would be dripping for me."

"You're wrong."

He steps closer, forcing my body back against the counter behind me. "Am I?"

"Stop it," I whisper, shaking my head.

"Just say the word, and I'll let you go."

He's challenging me. I hate that he's right. My body is alive for him, but I won't show him that. My pride won't allow it. I take a deep breath, straighten my shoulders, and growl, "Let me go."

He takes a step back, his eyes hazy and relaxed.

"If that's what you want, *inocencia*, but I don't offer twice," he rasps, and then turns and leaves the room.

Damn him.

He wasn't meant to make me feel like I made the wrong choice.

∼

"I have new sheets for you," Jess says, coming into my room the next day with a bundle of sheets in her hand.

I've been so desperately wanting to ask her why she's here, and after watching her flitter around the room, I finally get up the courage to blurt out, "Why do you do it?"

She's just placed the sheets on the sofa, but at my words she turns and stares at me, her green eyes confused. "Why do I do what?"

"Stay here . . . with them?"

She looks around the room a moment, as if double-checking that we are really alone, then she walks over and sits down on the sofa beside me. She places her hands in her lap, and stares at Hendrix's bed, just watching it for a long, long moment.

"He saved my life."

"Hendrix?" I say, shocked.

"Yeah, he saved me."

I don't say anything. I just stare at her, willing her to go on with my pleading look. She closes her eyes a moment, and then she begins speaking softly.

"I was a foster child, thrown through the system after my parents died when I was only four years old. I went through family after family, but my last family . . . they were awful. Well, one person in particular was awful . . . my foster father. He was abusive, and cruel, and one night . . . he raped me. I was twelve years old."

My chest seizes for her; everything inside my body clenches tightly, as if recoiling from the words.

"It went on for about four years. When I was sixteen, I lost it and I killed him. I was so tired of it, so drained. I wanted to be free. I wasn't thinking, I knew killing him wouldn't free me from my pain, but I had no other choice. It wasn't going to stop. One night, I tucked a knife under my pillow. When he came in, I stabbed him so many times he was unrecognizable. I ran, covered in blood and frantic. I ended up at the wharf, I don't know how, and I ran into Hendrix when he was docking to load his ship. I didn't know what he was—I just knew I was beside myself, and he calmed me down and managed to figure out what was going on through my babbling. He told me he would make me a deal. He would take me, hide me, and keep me safe, if I promised to become a medic on his ship. I had no medical experience, but he paid for some basic study, and the rest I figured out on my own. He told me after five years I could leave if I wanted; until then, I was under his protection."

He saved her? He took her on and saved her from a life in prison?

"Will you ever go back?"

She shakes her head. "The police would have me in an instant if I went back."

"And you're happy here?"

Her face falls. "The guys are like my family, but I know I'll never find love, or have children, or get married. That's just the life I've been handed."

"I'm so sorry," I say, gently.

She turns to me, forcing a smile. "It's nice to have another girl on here, aside from Senny. She's awful."

I chuckle softly. "She is awful, and I hope you and I can be friends."

She smiles, and it changes her face. She's a beautiful girl; it's such a shame she has to live this kind of life.

"You know, he's not an awful man."

"Hendrix, you mean?"

"Yeah, he's not cold-hearted. He just behaves that way."

"He's selling me . . ."

She frowns. "I don't understand why. I know he has a massive debt with the other pirates . . . I really hate that he is resorting to bartering someone's life, especially after he saved mine."

I swallow, and my body trembles as fear washes over me. I guess the reality of my situation hasn't sunk in. Hearing it from her . . . knowing it's real . . . it scares me. God, it scares me.

"I'm afraid," I whisper, looking down.

Jess surprises me by reaching over and gripping my hand. "Fight," she says softly. "Fight for your life, make him see it differently. He's not a horrible person. Give him a reason to keep you."

The door creaks, and she quickly lets go of my hand and stands. Hendrix steps in and stares at her with narrowed eyes, then turns his gaze to me. I give him a casual expression, and then turn my eyes to a magazine on the coffee table. Jess puts the sheets on the sofa and then rushes out. As soon as she's gone, Hendrix walks over, stopping in front of me. I focus on his boots, on the scuff marks up the sides.

"It's roast night in the dining room," he says. "You don't have to spend your days in here."

"Is my friend allowed to come?" I say, lifting my eyes.

"No, but you can take him food."

I shake my head and push myself to my feet. "Then I'm not interested."

I step past him and head for the door.

"I wanted to ask the other day, but . . . those scars on your . . . breasts. They're from him?"

I stiffen, and spin around. "What is on my body is none of your concern. I'm no more than a sale to you, pirate. Don't try to make out that this is anything more. Or is it just that you are worried about what my new owner will think of the damaged goods?"

"I want to know," he grinds out, "because I want to kill the prick for laying his hands on you."

"Why?" I bark, gripping the door. "You're no better than him."

Then I step out and slam it.

I hear him curse.

Jess's words play in my mind.

Give him a reason to keep you.

∼

"You're not seriously considering joining them?" Eric says, running his fingers through his matted blond hair.

Hendrix has allowed him to shower, but he still looks awful. I adjust my stance, rocking from one foot to the other. "I have to try, Eric. If I can make him . . . like me . . ."

"You're going to seduce him?" he rasps. "Aren't you?"

"I never said that, but I need to give him a reason to keep me, or at least reconsider his choice."

"And you're willing to sleep with him to get that?"

I cross my arms, and glare at him. "Sleeping with him would be a small price to pay for my life, don't you think? And I never said I was even going to do that, so stop jumping to conclusions."

"It's a stupid plan. He will simply get angrier and hurt you. Then where will you be? Or worse, he'll hurt me. Is that what you want?"

"Don't you dare," I spit. "I have signed my freedom away for you, Eric."

"And I'm stuck in a cell for you!"

My body stiffens, and my heart begins thumping angrily. I feel my eyes narrow with rage, and I lean in and grip the bars.

"How dare you," I snarl.

"If it wasn't for you not following the law, we wouldn't be here."

"Are you serious?" I scream.

"You should have let the police deal with Kane, and then we would have never felt the need to get on that yacht. I told you to leave it to the law, but you refused . . ."

My mouth drops open, and I feel my eyes well with tears. "You're my best friend, Eric. I have laid my life down for you, to keep you safe, but you know what? Fuck you. I'm doing this my way now."

I turn and head toward the door, my shoulders stiff, my heart aching.

"Indigo!"

I throw my rude finger up over my shoulder, and walk up the stairs.

Screw him.

Screw it all.

I'm going to try to have some fun.

CHAPTER NINE

Loot, plunder, pillage, and play!

"You're not scared of a girl, are ye?" I snort, standing in front of a group of three pirates who are looking at me like I've lost my mind.

"Not scared of no lady," one of the older ones says.

"Then let me join you."

They all raise their brows, and then look at each other.

"Aren't you a prisoner? We don't dance with prisoners, so to speak," the oldest of the group says.

"Hendrix and I have a deal. Besides, he invited me here tonight."

They raise their brows.

"Truth," I nod. "Now, who is going to give me a rum?"

They look at each other again, and then one of them thrusts a bottle of rum at me. The liquid sloshes over the mouth of the bottle and the smell burns the hairs in my nose. Jesus, what is in this?

"Sure you can handle it, lassie?"

I grin, and put my lips to the bottle, tilting my head back and taking a swig. It burns the entire way down, and the urge to cough is overwhelming, but I won't allow myself to show that. The liquid hits my stomach, and shit, it's lethal. I hand the bottle back, wink at the pirates, and then grab a stool and join them.

"So, tell me what your names are," I say, crossing my legs.

They give me odd expressions, before shrugging and answering me.

"Jock," says the first one, with long gray hair, a blue bandana, and more piercings than any man his age should have. He has them in his nose, his lips, his eyes, hell, even his eyebrows.

"GG," the second one says. He's the youngest, and has salt and pepper hair, a body covered in tattoos, and eyes so green they stand out like emeralds in his old, worn-out brown skin.

"Lenny," the third says. He's the kindest-looking of the three, with big brown eyes, wavy gray and brown hair, and a beard that nearly touches his chest.

"I'm Indigo, but you can call me Indi, or Lassie, or Poppet, or whatever the hell you want."

They grin.

I've broken the ice.

"You want another?" Lenny says, thrusting the bottle of rum at me.

My stomach twists in rejection of the idea, but I take it anyway, swallowing another lethal dose. Oh. Ew. Two sips later and my head is spinning. The alcohol percentage in this rum is strong.

"So, what were you doin' on the yacht out in the ocean anyway?" GG asks, lighting a cigarette.

"I was going to the United Kingdom. The boat caught fire, and we drifted. What were you pirates doing in those waters?"

"We just stocked up, so we had to pass through. It's dangerous waters, and we usually have to be quick. Picking you up was a risk," Jock says.

"Well, lucky for you it ended well." I wink.

"You're a firecracker, ain't ya, Indi girl?" GG says, smirking.

"I can be. Now, tell me, are you for real pirates?"

They all raise their brows.

"Seriously," I slur a little. "I mean, I thought pirates were fictional."

GG chuckles. "There ain't nothin' fictional about us, Indi girl."

"Okay, so . . . is there like some big story behind it? Your papa's granddaddy was a pirate . . . it's in your blood . . ."

They all shake their heads.

"Ain't no different to a motorcycle club on the land. We're like them, but ocean-style."

"The rebels of the ocean." I grin.

Jock laughs. "Exactly. We just do our business out here. Less laws."

"Smart thinking, Ninety-nine."

GG snorts, and hands me the bottle of rum again. I take it, swallowing it far more easily this time around.

"How long have you been with Hendrix, then?" I say, leaning back and feeling myself sway.

"Ten years, maybe more," GG says.

"That's a long time. You are all older than him. Isn't that weird?"

"Hendrix started his own crew, and he gave us all freedom by taking us on. We all have our own problems, our own secrets, and he lets us escape them. Young or not, he gave us something we couldn't find on the shore."

They make a valid point.

"So, do you, like, talk 'pirate'?"

GG raises his brows. "No, love."

"Well, that's no fun. I think I need to introduce that to ye scallywags."

They all burst out laughing.

"I see you decided to join in like I suggested," comes a husky, sexy voice from behind me. Oh damn.

I turn and grin up at Hendrix. "Aye, Cap'n, I took yer advice and joined in this party."

He raises his brows. "Seriously?"

"Arrrr, seriously."

GG laughs so hard he snorts, and that gets Jock going.

Hendrix raises his brows at me, and oh, he's so gorgeous standing there, looking down at me. His dark hair is all ruffled, and I want to put my fingers in it and tug, I want to hear him growl. He's so damned yummy; it's rude to be that perfect.

"Have you been drinking?"

"Arrrrr, I have had a clap of thunder or two with these scallywags. And they haven't yet drawn their cutlasses and sent me down to Davy Jones' locker."

Hendrix's lips twitch, and my heart swells. Maybe Jess is right. Maybe there is a chance of changing his mind. Jock is laughing so hard he falls backward off his chair, and it smashes loudly onto the floor. I watch as another group of pirates come into the room, the group that bothered me up on deck. They stare over at me, then at the men laughing, and their expressions seem to soften. Drake notices me, and I watch his eyes light up. I wave to him like a crazy lunatic.

"Hey, Drake!"

Hendrix turns and stares at Drake, then turns back to me.

"I'm guessing dinner will be a good thing. You've had far too much to drink."

"Nay, Cap'n. I am just getting started. Ahoy!"

He shakes his head, pulls out a cigarette, and lights it. He turns and walks over to the large table at the back of the room, then sits down at it. A moment later, Senny saunters in, wearing a pair of too-tight jeans and a top that has her breasts overflowing. I watch as she slides onto the table in front of Hendrix and says something that has him chuckling. Oh Lordy, when he smiles, he has these killer dimples. My heart begins thumping, and my head spins, giving me a light airy feeling.

"Is there any music on this here ship?" I say, turning back to the guys.

GG nods and stands, walks over to a large stereo in the corner. He flicks it on, and moments later, some ridiculous seventies music comes blaring out. I raise my brows, horrified.

"Seriously, seventies?"

GG shrugs. "It's the radio, Indi girl. We don't control it."

"Boo!"

I stand and walk toward the door. I really need to pee.

"Going already?" Hendrix says, just as I reach it.

I turn, meeting his gaze dead on. "Oh, I'll be back—don't you worry your pretty head about that."

His lips twitch again.

I'm softening the shell . . .

I stumble out the door and stagger down the hall until I find Hendrix's room. I walk in, hitting four walls before reaching the bathroom. When I'm done, I wash my hands and head back out to see Drake standing at the door. He smiles at me.

I smirk. "The boss man sent you to make sure I didn't drop over the side of the ship."

Drake walks over, hooking his arm through mine. "Yeah, something like that."

"Well then, Drakey boy, let's get this party started. Do you want to hear a joke?"

He snorts. "Not really."

"I'm telling you anyway. Why can't a pirate watch a horror film?"

He shakes his head, smirking. "You're about to tell me."

"Because it's rated ARRRRRR!"

He chuckles. "That's the worst pirate joke I've ever heard."

"Oh, oh, oh, I have another one. Why are pirates awesome?"

He doesn't answer; he just shrugs.

"They just ARRRRR!"

Laughing, we walk back to the dining room. When we step in, Hendrix appears in front of us. "She causing problems, buddy?" he asks Drake.

"If you call bad pirate jokes problems, then sure."

Hendrix raises his brows at me. "Bad jokes, eh?"

"You want to hear one?" I cry, removing my arm from Drake and putting it through Hendrix's. He stiffens, like he's shocked, but I don't give him a chance to react.

We join the other guys, and I sit in the middle on the floor. GG hands me another shot, and I clap my hands together, shooting it back before beginning my jokes again.

"You boys want to hear the best joke?"

GG nods, chuckling "Go on, hit us with your best shot."

"Why do pirates wear eye patches?"

GG shrugs.

"Because they can't afford iPads!"

GG snorts and Drake chuckles.

"That the best you got, *inocencia*?" Hendrix purrs.

I crack my knuckles. "I'm just getting started, pirate. Why did the pirate go on vacation? He needed some ARRRR and ARRRR!"

Hendrix rolls his eyes.

"I'll make you laugh, pirate," I vow. I wiggle on the floor, and cross my legs. "What's a pirate's favorite doll?"

Hendrix's eyes are dancing with amusement as he shrugs.

"A BARRRBIE!"

He snorts, and a lazy half grin appears on his face.

It's working.

~

"Oh my God!" I squeal, standing and spinning in a big circle. I am so drunk I can't see straight, but I haven't had so much fun in years.

I shouldn't be having fun, this I know, but I have to believe there is hope for me if I get to know the crew. Maybe Hendrix will change his mind. Maybe he'll let me go, or he'll keep me here. I'd rather spend my life here than as someone's slave. I have a better chance of escape.

"I love this song!"

I spin in the middle of the dining room while the rest of the crew eat. I dance and twirl, completely oblivious to the people around me. I'm having the time of my life. I begin singing at the top of my lungs, waving my hands around. I spin too fast and trip, landing on my ass so hard I bellow a curse and fall backward, flopping onto the floor like the tragic drunk girl I am. We girls are really classy drunks.

"Think it's time for you to go to bed," Hendrix says, suddenly appearing above me.

"You're beautiful, do you know that? Oh yes, you ARRRRRRR," I slur, squinting my eyes and taking him in. "Ohhh, so beautiful."

He shakes his head and leans down, wrapping his fingers around my arms and pulling me up with one quick movement.

"You're drunk. Come on, before you hurt yourself."

"Would you save me, c . . . c . . . c . . . Cap'n?" I chuckle.

"Unlikely, you're a messy drunk."

"Dance with me, buccaneer?" I giggle, spinning and wrapping my arms around him. He stiffens, and reaches back, gripping my hands and leaning down close.

"No. Now come on—quit while you're ahead."

"Fun spoiler."

He gives me a look, and then turns us both and leads me out of the dining room. I can't lie and say I don't enjoy the feeling of having his arms around me, drunk or not. When we get to his room, he walks me in and takes me over to the sofa, gently dropping me down. I flop back, giggling.

"Were you impressed by my pirate jokes?" I grin.

He grins at me. "You should have been a comedian. Now go to bed."

"I don't want to. This might be the last night of fun I'll ever have."

His eyes grow serious, and he stares down at me. "Sleep, *inocencia*."

I shake my head and lean back, staring up at him. "How did you become a pirate?"

He tilts his head to the side and watches me for a moment, before pulling out a flask and taking a swig.

"I got tangled up in some bullshit when I was fifteen. I had some things go down and eventually, when I was about twenty-five, I started forming a crew. Being out on the ocean away from it all . . . it made me feel free. I also realized running illegal stuff was easier out here, and so here we are."

"And it's okay with you, to live a life on a ship?"

"A life is only as good as you make it."

"So wise." I giggle.

He shakes his head, digging around in his pockets until he finds a cigarette. He lights it, bringing it to his lips and inhaling. Why does he look so good when he does that? I watch him for long moments, just inhaling and exhaling the smoke.

"You need to get some rest," he says, lowering his cigarette.

He stubs it out on the ashtray sitting on the coffee table, and then he turns and goes to walk out.

"The scars are from him," I blurt out.

He stops and turns, staring down at me.

"How long?"

I know what he's asking: How long was he beating me?

"Over two years."

"He got charged?"

"Yes," I hiccup. "After I shot him. He threatened me when he got out, so I got on a yacht and ran . . . and here I am."

Hendrix stares at me, his eyes holding an expression my drunken mind can't read. "And he's after you?"

I shrug. "I don't know. If he is, he won't find me here."

He makes a grunting sound, and then goes to turn away again.

"Hendrix?" I call, my voice loud and high-pitched.

He turns back to me.

"I don't think you're as bad as you think you are."

His eyes search my face, and his jaw flexes. "You don't know me."

"Would you let me know you?"

He studies my face, and then turns and walks to the door. Just before he gets to it, he murmurs, "no," and then steps out and closes it behind him.

Well, he can "no" me all he likes.

I'm not giving up.

CHAPTER TEN

Shiver me timbers!

I blink, and my head spins. It's dark and I can't see a thing. I need to pee, but the idea of getting off this sofa is really not appealing. I manage to struggle up into a sitting position, and I try to reach forward for the coffee table. I reach too far in the wrong direction and end up crashing onto the ground with a loud squeal. I fumble around on the floor. Goddammit, I can't see. My head is still spinning and I am disoriented. I pat the ground, trying to find something to give me an indication of where I am.

I touch a set of feet.

Oh.

Hendrix.

If I wasn't drunk, I'm sure I wouldn't have done what I do next, but I am drunk, so I blame that. I reach up, as if going for his hand, only to grab his cock. I literally grip hold of it, and wrap my fingers around it. He hisses. I realize what I've done, and I squeal and launch myself backward, landing against the coffee table with a cry. Hendrix is there in a second, lifting me into the air. I fall into him, wrapping my fingers around his arms.

I stop breathing.

I'm almost sure he does, too.

His body is pressed against mine, and I force myself to take one little moment to feel every inch of it. His hard, bare chest is warm against my cheek, and he smells divine. His abs are pressing against my belly, and I can feel them flexing. His arms are firm and strong beneath my fingers and his . . . oh . . . oh, my . . . his cock is hard. My head spins, and my body heats all over as I feel him pressing against my pelvis, and when he pulses, my world spins. Shit. Fuck.

I want him.

I lift my head and turn it, before lowering back down and pressing my lips to his chest. I don't know why I do it. I know I shouldn't. I should be pretending to seduce him, not actually enjoying it. He tenses all over. His skin is so goddamned hot, and I can't resist the urge so I slide my tongue out and taste the flesh there. Oh. *Lovely.* Hendrix has his hand on my hip. I didn't even notice until now, but that hand moves down until he's gripping my ass. His fingers bite into my skin as he jerks me forward, lowering his body just enough so that my pussy rides against his erection.

I groan.

He snarls.

And then he begins to grind.

Everything in my world stops. My head is spinning, my body is tingling all over, and my pussy is so damned wet I can feel my arousal dampening my panties. Hendrix grips my ass harder, and he rubs his erection up and down the thin layer of cotton over my sex. All I'm wearing is a long shirt and panties. I must have managed to change myself during the evening some time. I spread my legs a little, and my core begins to heat with each grind of his hips.

"I can feel you. You're so fucking wet," he whispers. I just barely hear him.

I whimper, and he rubs harder, faster, his hips gyrating against mine, and his cock sliding up and down my slit, causing the perfect friction. I want to come; I need to come. My nails grip his arms so tightly I feel the skin break, which only makes him wilder. He makes a throaty, hissing sound and I drop my head back. I'm close, so damned close. I can't think of anything but the heat pooling low in my belly. I want to go over that edge . . .

Hendrix rotates his hips, and then presses them so close, forcing his erection to press against my clit, hard. I come, shamefully loud. I cry out, and my body shakes as I begin convulsing. Each shudder goes through my body and causes it to jerk. It feels so good, God, it feels so fucking good.

Hendrix pulls back, and I hear him shuffling. He grips my hand, and suddenly my fingers are wrapped around a hard, very large cock. He curls his hand around mine, and he makes us stroke together.

Five solid pumps later, he lets out a guttural moan, and I feel the hot spurts of come hit my hand and roll down my wrist. I whimper, and my pussy clenches knowing he got so aroused. I lift my head, and my knees threaten to give way. I can smell the alcohol on my breath, or is it his? I don't know. We have both had too much. He steps back, curses loudly, and then I can't feel him anymore. I stand in the darkness, trembling and alone.

"H . . . H . . . Hendrix?" I whisper.

I hear the door slam.

And I know he's gone.

Well, shit.

What does that mean?

I am fairly sure my head has never hurt so much in my life. When I wake in the morning, it's pounding. I go to sit up, and it spins angrily, causing me to drop back down with a groan. Jesus, why the hell did I drink so much? Whose genius idea was that? I rub my temples and try to give myself an encouragement talk to hype myself for the idea of getting up. I need water, and I need aspirin. I am pretty sure both are equally as important as the other.

I hear the sound of a glass being placed on the coffee table beside me, and I turn my head to see Drake staring down at me. He raises his brows when I groan and clench my eyes shut. "Hendrix said you might need these."

Hendrix.

Oh.

God.

We fooled around last night. Shit, that sounds so childish. *Fooled around.* It wasn't even serious—it was just a drunken bump and grind. We both wanted it, though, that was clear. Did my attempt at seduction work? Do I actually have a chance to seduce Hendrix and make him reconsider his decision to sell me? My heart swells with hope, but quickly crashes. He did rush out, and he's not here this morning. I pout and open my eyes to stare up at Drake, who is still watching me.

"Where is he?"

He gives me a confused look. "Hendrix?"

"Yeah, Hendrix."

"He's on deck."

I nod, and slowly rise off the sofa. Drake leans down and grips the glass, raising it and extending his hand toward me. I take it gratefully, and I reach out for the aspirin, popping it into my mouth and swallowing it with water. God, my stomach is twisting and I feel seedy as hell. I'm never drinking that toxic rum again. I put my head in my hands again. My lord, it's thumping.

"A shower and fresh air always help a hangover. Maybe some decent food."

I lift my head from my hands and stare up at Drake. "Thanks."

"Your friend asked for you this morning when I delivered his food; he said it was urgent."

I sigh. I know Eric wants to talk to me after our fight, and I know I can't escape him forever. "I'll eat, and then I'll go and see him."

"Breakfast is still on in the dining room."

I get to my feet, and my knees wobble. My head pounds and my eyes feel as though they're about to drop out. "Thanks," I mutter.

"It's lethal stuff."

I stare at him, and I swear he looks like he wants to smirk. "No shit."

He does smirk now, and it transforms his entire face. His eyes change, and he's got one cute dimple in his cheek. It's odd; most people have two. I can't help but return his odd smirk, and, with no words needed, we both turn and walk away. I head to the shower and spend the next half an hour in it, relieving some of the pain in my hung-over body. When I'm done, I throw on a pair of jeans and a tank and head toward the dining room.

The chef is just clearing up when I come in, but he offers me a bowl of fruit. I take it, grateful, and pick at the juicy green melon as I head down to see Eric. I'm really not looking forward to this confrontation, but I know it has to be done. I can't imagine he's doing so well down in the cells, and I know it must be sending him a little crazy. He needs me, regardless of how we're both feeling, and I won't leave him in his time of need.

Midway down the hall a ladder suddenly swings down from the roof, and GG appears. I squeal and leap backward, then cry out when my head pounds at the quick, jerky movement. GG grins and tilts his head to the side. "You look like shit, Indi girl."

I put my hand to my heart and peer up at the small hole leading into the roof. "Where the hell did you just come from?"

GG grins and slides the ladder back up into the roof. "It's the fire escape."

Fire escape.

Fire escape.

My head spins.

"Where does it go?" I try to ask casually.

"Up into the navigation office."

On the deck. Oh my. When we are close to an island I could get Eric and we could escape through it. We could jump over the side from the navigation office. Could that be our escape? Hope swells in my chest, and I try to nod casually as GG slides a latch across and then crosses his arms and turns to me. "You heading down to see your friend?"

I nod, picking out another piece of melon even though my stomach is churning. I grip it, and groan quietly. "Yeah, he requested me."

"Get some fresh air after. It helps."

"You all keep saying that," I force a smile, stepping past him.

"We speak from experience."

I laugh softly, and continue toward the cell door. I flick it open when I reach it, and head on down. Eric is fresh this morning, like he's been allowed to shower. He's sitting on a mattress that wasn't there before, and he's got some clean clothes. Hendrix has looked after him. Why? He never promised to do anything but feed him. Did our moment actually pay off? Eric looks up when I step into view, and he seems to sigh with relief.

"There you are. I was so worried," he says, standing and walking over to the bars.

"Drake said you wanted to see me," I say, popping a piece of pineapple into my mouth.

"Look, what I said last night—it was wrong. I didn't mean it, Indi. You know I didn't. I was angry, and scared, and I took it out on you. I care about you, and I care about what happens to you. I don't want you to be sold, and the idea of it has my entire body twisting in panic."

"I've got it covered. I told you that," I whisper.

"Do you honestly think your plan of seduction will work?" he almost hisses.

I wrap a hand around the bars and lean in close. "It already is. You got extras this morning, didn't you?"

All the blood drains from Eric's face. "You . . . you . . . slept with him?!"

I lean in closer. "No," I whisper. "I didn't, but . . . I'm creating a connection."

"It's a bad idea, Indi."

"It's the only one I have. I found a way off the ship, but if for some reason that fails, I need a backup plan. Him having feelings for me is my backup plan. I need to be sure that if there's no other way out, he won't sell me."

"It's risky," he murmurs, looking at the floor.

"Have you got anything better?"

He shakes his head, then suddenly reaches through the bars, gripping my wrists. "I care about you Indi, you know I do. I don't like the idea of you . . . seducing him to keep yourself safe."

"He's not so bad," I say gently.

Eric's eyes widen. "You care about him, don't you?"

"I never . . ."

"How stupid are you, Indigo? He's a monster. He's going to sell you as a sex slave. How the hell can you possibly see him as anything but the revolting pig he is?"

"He's got a reason for doing what he's doing, but he's not a bad person. I've seen it."

"You're just blinded because of his good looks, but there's much more to him than that. He's not going to soften, and you're wasting your time."

I tug my wrists from his. "You're my best friend Eric, and I love you, but don't make me regret my decision to save you."

His mouth drops open, and he stumbles backward. "How could you even say that?"

"Probably for the same reasons you said awful things to me."

"Indi . . ."

"I'm going. I don't want to say anything more. I said I'd get us off here, and you need to trust that I can."

I turn on my heel and walk off. Neither of us says another word. I need some fresh air.

I need to think.

CHAPTER ELEVEN

Blow me down!

As soon as the salty wind hits my face, I sigh and close my eyes. Oh, they were right; this is nice. I step up out farther onto the deck, and, carried on the salty breeze, I smell a touch of rain. I open my eyes and see a puff of dark clouds rolling in from the horizon. Is that a storm? My heart skitters, and I feel a whoosh of wind tickle my face. I hear voices trailing out from the navigation hut, so I walk over.

"It's a big one. We need to dock for the night," I hear Hendrix say.

"We're over two hundred miles from the nearest island, Cap," Drake adds.

"And we might only have hours before this hits," Lenny says.

"We have to head as close to land as possible, in case of capsizing."

Capsizing.

What?

My heart seizes, and I blink rapidly. Surely not? I mean, they've been out here for years and years. We're not going to capsize . . . are we? I wrap my arms around myself and rub, suddenly feeling cold.

I hear the creak of the door, and turn to see the guys heading out. Hendrix notices me, and his eyes widen for a second before locking with mine. A lot passes between us, and there's a long, heated pause before he says, "I guess you heard?"

I nod.

"Best you stay below deck."

"Are we going to . . . sink?" I whisper.

"Not if I have any say in it. We're heading toward a small island northeast of us. It's a distance away, but with a good wind we can make it. Go below deck."

"I wanted to speak . . ."

"Below deck, Indigo. Now."

I feel my eyes widen. He's become determined. He's giving me a look that's telling me not to argue, but more than that, it's telling me that I'd best not bring up last night. I nod and turn, walking toward the door. The wind makes a howling sound, and my skin prickles. I hope he's right, I hope we can make it to land before this storm hits. The idea of being stuck on a ship in a storm with the chance of capsizing isn't really something I want in my life right now.

I head below deck and think for a moment about going to warn Eric about the storm, but decide against it. It's not that I don't care about him. It's just that, right now, I'm confused, and even a little hurt, and it's easier if I just leave it. He needs space, and the truth is I'm afraid of what this is going to do to our friendship. He's angry with me, and I'm signing my life over to save his. The sad thing is, even if I was mad at him, and hated him, I could never let his life be taken because of me.

I run into Jess just outside Hendrix's room, and she gives me a warm smile. She looks so calm. Doesn't she know about the storm? I must look worse than I realize, because she narrows her eyes and places the sheets she's carrying on the ground before walking over and gripping my shoulders. "Are you okay?"

I shake my head weakly. "I . . ."

My voice cracks, and I realize how much I've been holding in. Damn Jess for getting it out of me. It's those big green eyes and the gentle features on her face. She's just that kind of person; she makes you want to curl up and cry, just so she'll hug you. She's kind of addictive. I let my body relax into hers just a little, and she rubs my shoulders gently, giving me a comforting feeling.

"What's happening? Come on, come into my room and talk to me. I have a few minutes."

I nod, and she leads me down the hall to her room. When we get in, I peer around. She has a small room, like most of the guys, but hers is cleaner and cozier. There's a small bed, not quite a single size, in the corner and an old, wooden desk by the small rounded window. I walk over to the bed and sit down. She has a faded pink comforter covering it, and I have the sudden urge to wrap myself in it.

"Is it Hendrix?" she asks, sitting down beside me.

"Last night . . . I got drunk and . . . God . . ."

"What happened?" she asks, turning toward me and crossing her legs on the bed. I do the same until we're facing each other.

"Well, I took your advice and decided to join in and get to know the crew. I got a little drunk and Hendrix took me back to his room. We didn't sleep together, but . . ."

"But," she urges, her big green eyes wide.

"We . . . fooled around."

"Fooled around how?"

My cheeks grow rosy, and I stare down at my hands. "I . . . oh God, I can't say it."

"It's nothing I haven't heard or experienced on this ship, Indi."

"It was all hands . . ."

Her eyes widen. "You got him off . . . with your hands?"

"Kind of. And grinding. It was an extremely erotic moment, and then afterward he turned and stormed out."

"You're his captive," she says gently. "He's freaking out. Don't give up. The fact he let you get close to him . . ."

"It's not like it's hard," I interrupt.

Jess shakes her head. "It is hard, Indi. The only reason he fucks Senny is because he needs something out here. There's no connection, and he sure as hell doesn't care about her. She's easy—it's as simple as it gets."

"Do you suppose he thinks I'm easy, too?"

She shakes her head. "No, he looks at you differently."

"How so?"

She shrugs, tucking a long, thick lock of hair behind her ear. "He just does. He watches you, and his eyes seem to glaze over. He's interested: there's a spark for him. Don't give up."

I cling to her words, because they give me a small moment of hope.

"I saw him earlier and he refused to talk about it. There's a storm coming, so I think his mind is elsewhere."

"Oh, I hope so."

I scrunch my brow in confusion. "You hope so?"

"If there's a storm, we get to dock on some pretty islands. We get a few days of swimming and peace before we have to get back on this ship. I crave those days."

"It does sound kind of nice, but I'm scared . . ."

She reaches across and takes my hand. "Don't be. Hendrix always gets us out before it starts."

"He said the island is a fair way away."

She smiles. "It's okay; I promise."

I hear the howling of the wind outside, and I detach my fingers from Jess's and wrap my arms around myself. I hope she's right; I'm not a huge fan of thunder. It's kind of my weakness.

"I should get back to work. Go through my drawers and find yourself a jacket so that you don't get cold. The wind will be freezing."

"Thanks, Jess."

She smiles. "Anytime. I'm always here."

When she's gone, I walk over to the window and watch the clouds rolling in. I'm off in a world of my own when a snarly voice fills my quiet space.

"Scared, princess?"

I turn and see Senny staring at me. I shake my head, refusing to answer her. I walk out of Jess's room and shove past her. This doesn't deter her; she follows me down the hall.

"Storms kill people out here."

No shit.

"Is there something you want, Senny?" I mutter.

"I just thought you had the right to understand the situation we're in."

"Hendrix and Jess have made it very clear," I point out, continuing my path down the hall.

"Ohhh," she coos. "Hendrix is looking after his little slave."

I stiffen and turn. "I don't know what your problem is, Senny, but I suggest you take it elsewhere."

"My problem is you," she growls.

"Again, I suggest you take it elsewhere. I'm not interested."

"Do you really think you're of any importance on this ship?"

"More so than you."

Her fists clench and her back straightens. "I've been here for longer than you, and let me tell you something, princess," she growls, stepping forward and getting into my face. "I'll be here long after."

Then she storms past me, leaving me to wonder if she's right.

The wind howls, and the ship rocks from side to side. I wrap my arms around myself, and my heart thumps wildly. I'm frightened. For the past two hours I've watched the storm come closer; I've watched the waves rise and crash against the side of the ship. I've watched the lightning hitting the water and making a sound so loud my ears are throbbing in pain. Eric is above deck now, and we're all in the dining room, waiting for the ship to come close enough to the island.

Jess is huddled up beside me, her hand firmly in mine. Eric has his arms around me, and he's holding me tightly, so tightly I can hardly breathe. I'm not sure if that's because it's been over a week since we've touched, or if it's because he's scared. The other pirates even seem to have a level of concern on their faces. Some of them are pacing, some drinking, some chatting frantically amongst themselves. We're all waiting on Hendrix, who has been in the navigation office now for twenty minutes with Drake, trying to get us closer.

"Do you think he's okay?" I whisper to Jess.

"He's okay. He doesn't come in usually, not until he's got an answer, at least."

"I hope something hasn't happ—"

I'm cut off because GG yells out, "Here he is!"

We turn and see Hendrix come through the dining room door. He's soaked and he's shivering, likely from a mix of adrenaline and cold. He walks over to us all and quickly scans the room. His eyes fall on mine, and our gazes lock, before he lifts his head and announces our plans. "We're close enough to get off, but it won't be easy. Buddy up; we're going off the left side. Take something each— a blanket, a bag, a tent, I don't care. Just take something. The ship is close enough for us to anchor, but we're going to have to wade through some water. We have ten, maybe fifteen minutes before the storm hits the island, if we're lucky. I've managed to get south of it, for the moment. GG, you're taking the prisoner."

I feel Eric stiffen beside me. "I'll take Indi. She knows me."

Hendrix spins to him, and the look on his face is that of pure rage. "You're not in any position to argue with me, boy. The girl comes with me."

The girl.

The girl.

That burns. Why does it burn?

"I'll go with someone else, I'm not doing anything with you," I say, my voice wavering.

Hendrix storms over, leaning down and meeting my gaze. "We've danced this dance before, *inocencia*," he murmurs. "It's time for some new moves. We don't have time for this. You're coming with me because you're safest with me. Your little hero over there will drown you in a split second."

He lifts his head, leaving me struggling for calm. "Move!"

The pirates scatter. Drake takes Jess, GG takes Eric, and they all buddy off and rush out. Hendrix takes my arm and pulls me out of the dining room. We power down the halls, him dragging me and me concentrating on making my legs move in time. He stops by his room, grips a rolled-up sleeping bag from under the bed, and throws it over his shoulder. Lightening crackles in the background, and I begin to tremble.

"I'm afraid," I cry suddenly, before I can stop it.

Hendrix stops, and turns. Surprising me, he reaches down and grips my face. "You're just fine with me, okay? Just do as I ask. You'll be okay."

I nod, chewing on my bottom lip like a maniac. He turns and pulls me up on deck. As soon as we step out, the rain crashes down over us and soaks us to our cores. I am shivering in seconds, and dodging people as Hendrix drags me toward the exit. I can hear tree branches snapping as the wind whips through, and I know we're right on the island. Hendrix pulls out a flashlight and flicks it on. It's obviously waterproof because it doesn't flicker off.

He leads us over to the side of the ship, and I can't see anything. All I can do is listen. I hear waves crashing against the side of the ship, and it's rocking angrily. Pirates are climbing down the ladder and wading through the water, and I'm almost sure I catch a glimpse of Eric. Hendrix wraps an arm around me, and before I know what's happening, he pulls us over the side of the ship. I try as best I can to keep up with him and follow his instructions, but it's near on impossible.

The wind is too strong.

The waves are too deadly.

We hit the water with a crash, and somehow Hendrix manages to keep his arm around me. I cling to him now. I no longer care about acting strong. I wrap my arms and legs around him. The water is beyond freezing, to the point that it burns my skin, like someone is sticking me with tiny little pins. The salt burns my eyes as the waves crash over our heads. We surface, and I'm coughing so violently I'm fairly sure I'm about to lose a lung.

"Good girl," he yells over the wind. "Hold onto me."

I do.

I hold on as tightly as I can. He wades through the water, pulling against the waves. All I can think about is the fact that, at any second, lightning could hit the water and kill us all. It's like I'm counting down the minutes, my chest seizing with fear, only I don't know if and when it's going to happen. My tears mix with the salt, and my lungs burn from the amount of water I've inhaled. I'm so cold I'm shaking, and the wind is so loud I can hardly hear anything over it.

"Nearly there. Good girl," Hendrix says into my ear, in a soothing tone.

He's soothing me.

Oh, God. He's soothing me.

When I feel the sand beneath us, I drop my feet only to put one foot down on something sharp. I cry out, lifting it back up. A burning pain shoots up my leg, and my foot begins to throb.

"Shit, did you cut yourself?"

"Yes," I cry.

"Just keep your legs around me. Don't put them down, Indigo."

I lift my legs back up around his waist, and he continues fighting the wind and the rain until we're finally on the sand. He doesn't stop. He runs up toward the trees, the flashlight in one hand, the other hand hooked around me. I don't know why he still has the sleeping bag over his shoulder; it's no doubt soaked. He weaves through the trees, and I hear the sound of voices ahead.

"We have a cover, Cap, a cave," someone calls.

"Thank fuck," he yells. "Is everyone here? Shout out your names."

One by one, they all call their names. When I hear Eric's, my entire body goes weak. I can hear the crunching of boots, and I can see a faint light ahead. Every now and then I catch a glimpse of a face when Hendrix flashes his light. There's still a few running toward the cave.

"I need a shirt, something to tie her foot. She cut it," Hendrix orders.

"Here, Cap."

A moment later, a shirt is thrust toward us from the darkness. Hendrix catches it, and then shines the flashlight toward the dull light coming from the distance. He runs toward it just as the first crack of lightning hits the tree behind us. I scream, and he moves quicker, until he basically slides us into the small cave. As soon as the rain stops pounding against my skin, the shivering becomes violent. Hendrix lowers us down against the wall of the cave until we're both on the ground. I can hear the rustling and frantic chatting around us, but I can't focus on it, I'm shaking so hard.

"You're fuckin' freezing," Hendrix murmurs, shifting me until I'm tucked into his side.

"We've got blankets, Cap."

"I got one," he says.

"It's s . . . s . . . soaked," I rasp.

"Waterproof cover," he says, placing the flashlight down, dropping the sleeping bag off his shoulder and then reaching for the shirt.

I hear a tearing sound, and then he shines the torch on my foot. I see blood as soon as it flashes across my skin, and I turn my eyes away quickly.

"Deep gash," he says, turning my foot from side to side.

I don't say anything; I just sit, shivering, as he ties the torn strip of shirt around my foot. When he's done, he shines the torch around the crew. "Everyone got something warm?"

They all mutter a "yeah."

"Get some sleep; this will be a long one."

He grips me and all our things, and slides us right to the far left corner where it's quieter. The wind is howling outside, and the rain is hammering down so hard I can hear the droplets against the stones. The thunder crackles through the sky, and I can hear the faint sounds of the crew members trying to talk over it.

"Shirt off," Hendrix says suddenly.

"What?" I rasp.

"You need to get those clothes off, trust me. You won't dry in here, and you'll freeze."

"But . . ."

"Just do as you're fucking told," he barks.

I quickly grip my shirt and pull it over my head, and then I discard my soaked jeans. Hendrix rips his shirt off, and shuffles out of his jeans, too, before opening the sleeping bag and rolling it out. He gets in, unzips it, and opens it up for me.

"Y . . . y . . . you want me to get in there . . . with you?"

"Survival. Trust me, I'm not happy about it either, but it works."

My teeth clatter together as I hesitate.

"Don't play with me, Indi. Just get in."

"Do it, Indi," I hear Jess say from the darkness. "Please."

"Indi," Eric pleads. "Don't."

"Oh for fuck's sakes," Hendrix grumbles, reaching out, gripping my arm and pulling me down.

I go easily. It's hard not to when you're so cold. He pulls me into his side and then throws the blanket over us. I stiffen for the longest moment, unable to feel anything but his cool body against mine, but that soon begins to turn warm and my shivering stops. Exhaustion washes over me, and I drop my head into his arm, smelling the seawater on his skin.

"Not such a stupid idea now, is it?" he murmurs.

"No," I whisper.

His fingers slide up my back, where he begins to rub my skin.

"Is your foot hurting?"

I concentrate for a moment on the ache in my foot; it's not too bad. "It's dealable."

"Try and get some sleep. This storm ain't going anywhere for tonight, and we usually have a solid day's work to tidy up the ship."

I nod into his shoulder, and close my eyes. As I begin to drift off, I begin sliding my fingers over the hard, warm muscles on his stomach. I don't realize I'm doing it; it's just a semi-conscious movement. My eyelids feel heavy, but my fingers keep moving, sliding up and down, around and around. It's only when Hendrix makes a throaty sound that I blink a few times, and realize my fingers are off in their own little world. I instantly stop them, and heat rises up in my cheeks. *Shit.*

"Don't stop," he whispers, so quietly I can barely hear him.

I start up the gentle stroking again, over and over, around and around, until I can feel him panting beside me, his body tight and firm. He's enjoying it, and when I shift and feel the throb between my legs, I realize I am, too. I roll slightly, and I feel his fingers splay out over my belly. Oh, God. Are we doing this? In the pouring rain, in a cave full of pirates? I bite my lip, knowing I should stop him, but also knowing I can't.

His fingers slide down lower, finding my panties. I hold my breath, and keep moving my fingers over his hard stomach. When he slides his fingers inside, I stiffen all over and bite my lip even harder to avoid crying out. He reaches down between my legs, parting my folds with his fingers before finding my clit. Oh. God. His thumb makes big, firm circles around the aching nub as his forefinger edges lower, finding my entrance that is already damp for him. Oh shit, I should be stopping this. I should be, but . . .

Oh, God.

He slides a finger inside me.

I stiffen all over, and his other hand grips my head, turning my face so it's pressed against his chest. He holds me there, making sure I don't scream and let the entire cave know he's got his finger deep inside me. He slides it out, before plunging it back in. My back arches, and my legs begin to quake. It takes every ounce of willpower inside of me not to scream. I'm biting my lip so hard I can taste blood, but I don't care. God, I don't care.

His thumb makes bigger circles, and, like a desperate, horny teenager, I plunge my hand into his boxers to find his erect cock. He stiffens, and sucks in a deep breath, but no noise escapes his throat. He begins fucking me harder with his fingers, circling my clit faster and faster. I match the pace with his cock. My hand works up and down frantically, desperately, wanting so much more. I'm on the edge, ready to go over. My entire body fills with warmth, and I can't hold back a second longer.

I turn my head, and release my lip before biting down onto the flesh on his chest. I come so hard my body jerks, and my teeth draw blood. I feel him stiffen, make a hissing sound, and then he's coming too, hot spurts of semen filling my palm. His body is rigid, mine is convulsing, yet we're both utterly silent. I release his chest, and slowly exhale a shaky breath as I slide my hand from his boxers. I find a stray corner of the blanket, and I wipe his release away.

He slides his hands from my panties, and I hear him suck my arousal off. I want to whimper and roll, straddling him and fucking him so damned hard that both of us pass out, but I know I can't. I just can't. I have to do this right. I have to know he wants me. We both lie in silence, and in a moment I resume my position against his chest, listening to his heart slowly stop thudding and I know . . . I just know . . .

What started out as a way of escape has just become something more to me.

Something so much more.

How the hell am I supposed to keep playing a game when I no longer care for the rules?

CHAPTER TWELVE

Hoist the colors!

I wake in the morning, and I feel a hard hot body pressing against mine. My entire body begins to tingle with the knowledge of Hendrix's presence. My stomach does a little somersault. I let my mind go back to what went on last night, and my cheeks flush. We got frisky in the sleeping bag, like two teenagers. Like it was forbidden and we weren't supposed to be doing it. Perhaps we weren't. That's why it feels like this. So wrong, so right—a mixture of emotions that blend in the oddest way.

I move gently, and Hendrix's arm slips off my stomach. He was holding me. Like I matter. I don't matter; we both know that. So why is he here protecting me? Is it purely because he wants to make this deal, and he doesn't want it to go bad if something happens to me, or is it because he cares more than he's letting on? Are my seductions actually working? Or is it a connection that was going to happen, no matter how things went down? I've felt a spark since the moment I laid eyes on him. Does he feel it, too?

I gently pull myself from the sleeping bag and get to my knees, peering around. I find the shirt I was wearing last night, and pull it on as well as my jeans. Everyone is sleeping, and I let my eyes fall on Eric, who is leaning against a rock looking awfully uncomfortable. I tilt my head and listen for rain. It's drizzling outside, but the urge to go out and breathe in the fresh air is far stronger than my hesitation over getting wet. I get to my feet and very carefully tiptoe out of the cave. The moment I straighten, I suck in a breath.

It. Is. Breathtaking.

There are no other words to describe it. Even through the drizzling rain and the rolling gray clouds in the sky, it's utterly gorgeous. The trees are thick, covered in a fine furry layer of moss. They range from tall and slim to short and bushy. The sound of birds chirping and bees buzzing fills the air. I can smell a mix of pine, salt, and fresh cool air. I shiver, and wrap my arms around myself as I take a step forward. I need to see more.

I walk out through the trees and peer over at the ship sitting on the sand. It looks as though it's been thrown up there without a care in the world. Seeing it like this makes me realize just how beautiful it really is. I had just pictured it as an old, raggedy ship. It's not. It's absolutely a work of art. It's massive, and the dark wood that it's made from really gives it something extra, like it just completes it. The flags are white, the detail in the wood is exquisite, and the mermaid on the front just tops it off. It's divine. I rub my arms and peer around at the beach. It's hard to see because of the fine layer of mist covering the water, but I already know that the water is blue and crystal clear.

I wiggle my toes in the damp sand and then head back toward camp, finding myself a small rock to sit on. I don't really want to go back into the cave; I just want some time to sit and think—preferably not about last night, because that would mean letting Hendrix back into my mind and the moment I do that, I'll start breaking out in shivers at the remembrance of how amazing it all felt.

"An early riser?"

Dammit.

I turn and see Hendrix standing, shirtless, leaning against a tree. He stares down at me with such intensity, I'm forced to look away. He walks over and sits himself down on the rock beside me. I don't look at him, probably because I'm afraid he'll see the feelings I'm battling if I do. He's quiet for a long while, so I figure maybe he's just out here to enjoy the view as much as I am.

"Sleep good?" he murmurs.

"Sure, as good as I could after that."

"Storms scare you?"

I shrug. "I'm not a fan."

"Why?"

I turn and stare at him. "I just . . . I don't know. I think it's the sound. When I was little, my dad used to hold me when the storms came close. After he . . ." I hesitate and look at Hendrix, ". . . left . . . it was never the same. I guess he was my comfort."

"Understandable," he says, staring out through the trees at the gorgeous ocean.

"What about you? Did you just learn to accept them after many years on the water?"

He shakes his head. "I fuckin' hate them. No matter how many times they come around, and they come around a lot, I still fear for my crew's lives. If we aren't close enough to an island, it can mean a horrible ending for us. The ship can't withstand a massive storm."

I never thought about it like that. It warms a small part of my heart to know he's worried about his crew. I knew they were important to him, of course, but I guess hearing him admit it scares him, is something new.

"I guess it's a good thing that you have reliable equipment so you are able to track them before they hit."

He nods. "But sometimes even the best technology fails, or it can be as simple as the fact that we are too far out to get to land."

"Have you ever been stuck in a storm?" I dare to ask, hoping I'm not invading personal memories that he doesn't want to share.

He nods but keeps his eyes on the ocean. "Once. The ship didn't upturn but we lost five men overboard trying to secure it."

My heart aches for him. His crew is without a doubt his family, so losing them would hurt as much as it would for anyone else to lose someone they loved.

"I'm sorry."

He turns and stares at me, like my apology confuses him. He quickly hides his shock and shrugs. "Life happens, people die. Especially out here."

"Yeah," I whisper. "I guess you're right."

"Anyway, I'm going to the ship to get some breakfast for the guys. You got a second to help?"

I nod and stand. He quickly does too and we make our way to the ship, which is shoved very roughly onto the sand.

"How'd it get onto the sand?" I ask, struggling to lift my feet. The sand is damp and heavy, and my foot is still aching.

"We anchor it down and it pretty much just launches itself up there with the waves."

That would explain why it looks as though it's literally been tossed onto the shore. Hendrix walks closer to it and slowly inspects the outside. There's no damage, thank God, but I'd imagine they won't be able to confirm that entirely until it's on the water. The bottom may have received some damage. Hendrix jumps up and secures a ladder, and then reaches down, offering me his hand. Hesitating for only a second, I take it.

We make our way through the ship, and I see quite a few things are upturned. Understandable, considering how hard it rocked. We go directly into the kitchen and stare at the mess on the floor. There are knives and cutlery that have just been flung around. Some plates and cups have smashed too. With a sigh, Hendrix steps through them and shoves the pantry open.

I walk over quickly, standing behind him. He turns with a handful of crackers, spreads, loaves of bread, and tinned beans. He puts a heap into my arms. I scrunch up my nose, causing him to stop and stare down at me. "What? Don't like what I'm puttin' in?"

"No . . . it's fine."

"Liar," he mutters. "Just say it, Indi. I know you want to."

"It's just . . . beans. Ugh."

He chuckles, warming my heart just a tiny bit more.

"Yeah, I'm not a fan myself but the guys love them."

"I know," I mutter. "I've heard them in the . . . ahhh . . ."

"In the john?"

I laugh softly. "Yeah."

"Welcome to life on a cramped ship."

He turns again after he's filled my hands and heads over to the fridge. He swings it open and pulls out a bottle of juice, some butter and fruit. Oh thank God. He places it all on the counter before rifling around until he can find some bags. When he does, he fills them up, taking the things from my arms and adding them too.

"Fruit good for you?" he asks, shoving the butter into the last bag.

"I love fruit."

"Most girls do."

"You don't?"

He wrinkles his nose. "Nah."

"What do you eat that's healthy, then?"

He turns to me, grinning. "Beans."

"You do not," I laugh.

He shakes his head. "No, I just stick with coffee in the morning."

"That's not healthy."

"No," he murmurs, handing me a bag. "I suppose it's not."

I shake my head with a smile on my face as we head off the ship. I guess it's because in that small moment together, where Hendrix didn't have his shield up, we actually learned something about each other. I'm trying hard to avoid letting that affect me, but it's very hard. He's affecting me with every minute that passes. And soon, there will be no turning back.

∼

After breakfast, I take the chance to escape on my own while everyone is sitting around a fire they managed to create with some dry wood Hendrix had on the ship. My foot is aching and I'm feeling the need to wash up, so I head toward the sound of running water. I trek through the trees, batting away mosquitoes and some other little flying insects, and keep on shoving through. I come closer to the water, and when I finally see the crystal-clear lagoon topped with a waterfall, I lose all my breath.

Oh.

My.

I didn't realize how cramped I'd been on the ship until this. The urge to strip off is strong enough that I find myself peering through the trees to make sure no one is around before gripping the hem of my shirt and pulling it up. I lift it off and toss it on the ground, and then discard my jeans. I hesitate with my bra and panties, but decide to leave them on. It's not worth the risk if someone decides to come down here. I find an entry point, and I slowly sink into the cool crisp water.

Oh, heaven.

I go under, letting the cool water soothe my slightly throbbing head. I make my way over to the waterfall, and little splatters of water and mist hit my face as I move closer. I climb up a few rocks, slipping a few times, before finally stepping underneath it. The water hitting my body is like an all-over massage. I groan and close my eyes, tilting my head back and letting it wash over me. It's almost erotic, like you need a body pressed up against you to make the experience that much more real.

I think about Hendrix, and the way his fingers fucked me last night. Shit, if he fucks that well with his fingers, I can't wait to see what he does with his cock. I shudder at the thought, and find my fingers grazing my nipples. They are hard, and a tingle shoots through my body when my fingers pinch the tips. A little moan escapes my lips, and the ache between my thighs intensifies. God, I haven't had sex for so long. At least a year. My body is desperate for it.

"Best get your fingers off those pretty nipples before I do something I'll regret."

The husky voice has me jumping back with a squeal. I slip on a rock, and feel my body going down, but a set of hard arms wraps around me and pulls me back up. I know it's Hendrix; what I don't know is how the hell he managed to sneak up on me. He was still at camp when I walked off. He must have followed closely behind. I open my eyes and look up at him. He's soaking wet, with all that dark hair sticking to his face. Damn him. He snakes his tongue out and licks a droplet of water off his lips, and realization hits. I've touched him, but he's not tried to kiss me.

Not once.

"I know what you're doin'," he murmurs, pressing a hand against my lower back and pulling me toward him.

"What's that?" I murmur.

"You're tryin' to seduce me."

I let my eyes scan his face, before muttering, "Don't flatter yourself. Maybe I actually want to do these things."

He grins, and reaches up, tangling a hand in my hair. "I don't usually fall for this shit, but fuck knows you're getting inside my head."

Oh. *Yes.*

"I'm not trying to make you fall for anything," I murmur, staring at his lips.

"You're in here, playin' with your nipples, half-naked and lookin' so fuckin' gorgeous it hurts. And you're tellin' me you're not playing with me?"

"That's what I'm telling you," I say, meeting his gaze. "I didn't know you were here, and I was . . . playing with myself, because the water felt nice on my body."

"Are you horny, little *inocencia*?" he purrs.

I think about my answer for a minute. This answer is going to push this over the line, or end it. Hendrix has just admitted that I am getting to him, which means there is something there. I started out with great hopes that his feelings would set me free, but if I were being truthful with myself, then I'd admit it's so much more than that. However, I'm not going to pass up the opportunity to watch him squirm, so I lean in closer and whisper, "I haven't been fucked for over a year, so yes, pirate, I'm horny."

He hisses, and he tugs on my hair. "You want me to fuck you, *inocencia*?"

"Do you want to fuck me, pirate?"

"You fuckin' know I do. There are conditions that come with it, however . . ."

I frown. "And what would they be?" I say, leaning up close so our lips are nearly touching.

Heat sizzles between us, and my entire body comes to life. Hendrix tugs at my hair, and my lips pull back. "The first, no kissing."

I shake my head in confusion. "What?"

"I don't kiss. It's personal, and I don't do it unless I am deeper with someone than just lust."

Ouch.

"Fine by me," I manage to stammer out.

"The second, we fuck once, and once only. I'm not going to be played with, and I know exactly what you're trying to do. I want to resist it, but I fucking can't. I need a taste. Just one fucking taste. You're not mine to claim, and I have a debt to pay."

Double ouch.

"Then why bother?" I hiss. "Don't bother trying to fuck me when it means no more than a bit of quick relief."

"You're tryin' to tell me your body isn't screamin' for that fuckin' release?" he growls.

Damn him. It is. So much so I don't actually care about the fact that he's only offering himself once. I'm alive for him; my entire body is tingling with need. Besides, if it's an explosive "one" time he might just change his mind.

"Fine," I say, leaning close. "No kissing, one decent fuck. We have a deal."

He grins. "Shall we put it in blood?"

"Bite me, pirate."

He chuckles, and then spins me around suddenly, pressing my back to his chest. "The third rule, we do it my way."

I shiver, giving him my answer in my reaction. He slides his fingers down my covered breasts, and I tremble beneath his touch.

"You want me to fuck you right here, right now?" he growls into my ear.

"Yes."

Nothing more needs to be spoken. He steps back and unclips my bra, before pressing himself back against me. His arms go around, and his fingers find my nipples. He gently twirls and pulls, rolling the hard buds between his fingers. I whimper, and my knees wobble. If he thinks I'm going to stay upright, he's very wrong.

"Have you ever been fucked against a rock wall, with a waterfall comin' down all over you?" he murmurs, sliding his lips over my shoulders.

"N . . . n . . . no," I stammer.

"Oh *inocencia*, you're in for a treat."

I feel my legs quiver, and I reach back and grip his arms, holding myself steady. "I . . . I'm not sure I can stay upright."

He pushes me toward the rock wall, and when we reach it he spins me around so my back presses against it. He dips his head, capturing my nipple in his mouth. I cry out, and my knees wobble. Oh, Jesus. His tongue flicks the tip, swirling and sending little bolts of pleasure through my body. He reaches down, finding my panties, and he slowly lowers them, sliding his mouth down my belly as he goes. Oh . . . yes.

When he's on his knees in front of me, and my panties are on the ground, he looks up. His eyes are fiery, and nearly black with need. He grips one of my thighs, and gently slides it to the left so my legs are spread. He makes a growling sound as he lifts a finger and swipes it through my damp sex. "So fuckin' sweet here, aren't you, *inocencia*?"

I don't answer him. I just drop my head back into the rock wall and close my eyes, letting myself enjoy every moment of this. Hendrix spreads my legs a little farther, and I can feel the water from the falls sliding down over my stomach and tickling my exposed clit. Sweet heaven, it's amazing. Hendrix leans in closer, and I can feel his hot breath against my most sensitive flesh before he plunges his tongue inside me.

I scream.

It comes so unexpectedly, that my body buckles. His hands reach up and grip my hips, stopping me from sliding down and landing in a heap on the ground. He plunges his tongue inside my flesh deeper, finding my clit and flicking it with ferocity. Then he gets it between his teeth, and begins rolling it with them. Holy . . . shit. A bolt of pleasure shoots through my body. It's so intense I find myself screaming out words I usually wouldn't use.

"Motherfucker," I groan.

Hendrix bites and rolls, licks and sucks, until I'm trembling all over and whimpering his name desperately. He removes one hand from my hip, and brings it down between us, finding my entrance and plunging two fingers inside. I come so hard I feel my eyes roll. I don't even realize my body has collapsed until I feel Hendrix stand us both up, and re-press my back against the wall. I hear his belt buckle, and I open my eyes to see he's looking right at me.

"Ready for this, *inocencia*?" he rasps.

"Yes," I almost plead.

He steps back for a second, and drops his belt. He unbuckles his jeans and yanks them down. When his cock springs free, I gasp. It's big. I mean, I knew it was, but seeing it like this, is just . . . wow. He wraps his fingers around it and begins gently stroking as he pulls a condom from his jeans pocket and tears it open with his teeth. With wide eyes, and an aching pussy, I watch as he rolls it down over the head of his cock, and then over the base. Naked, the man looks like he's meant to be a damned statue. He's so ridiculously perfect.

He steps forward when he's sheathed. He's got no shirt on, and like this, fully naked, he's heartwrenchingly breathtaking. I blink a few times, to make sure what I'm seeing is real. My reality becomes clearer when he presses himself against me, and his hands find my thighs. He grips them both, and lifts me, wrapping my legs around his waist. He reaches down between us, gripping his cock and guiding it to my entrance. My eyes roll again, and I drop my head into his shoulder.

"Look at me when I fuck you, *inocencia*," he orders.

I lift my head weakly, and meet his eyes. I've never watched a man during sex, but seeing the way his expression changes and his face softens as he slides inside me is something I'll never forget, or regret. He fills me slowly, stretching me. We both groan, and he releases one of my thighs to put his hand on the wall beside my head. I turn my gaze to his arm, and I watch it flex and pull as he tenses all over. Holy fuck. He's so damned yummy.

"So fuckin' tight," he rasps, clenching his jaw.

"Oh, yes," I cry out as he takes the final plunge, fully burying himself inside me.

"Jesus," he groans.

When he moves his hips, sliding out of me before plunging back in, everything in my world stops. It literally stops. I feel nothing but him. See nothing but him. I've never felt this in my entire life. I've never had someone take me to such a level before. He's literally changing everything. My eyes haze over as my body sparks to life. I've never had an orgasm during sex; the feeling building inside me is something I've never felt before.

"I . . . oh, God . . . what is that feeling?" I cry out, gripping his back and sinking my nails into his skin.

"You've never come before like this, sweetheart?" he pants, through gritted teeth.

"I don't . . . oh, God . . . Hendrix . . ."

"Oh baby, fuck. Let me be the first, let me take you over that edge."

I shake my head from side to side as bolts of pleasure shoot up my core and settle low in my belly. Oh. God. I can feel my entire body clenching around him, tightening, hanging on that edge. Is this it? What everyone raves about? Hendrix drops his head into my neck, where he begins to suckle gently. Oh fuck. Oh my God. I rasp out his name, and my desperate whimpers turn into pathetic little screams for more. Hendrix moves his hips faster, filling me even deeper until I'm on that edge, ready to go, just needing that push.

My fingers are warm with the blood from his back. I'm scratching him, and I don't even care. He reaches between us, finding my clit with his thumb. He rubs the wet nub, swirling my arousal around and around, pressing on and off it, taking me to the edge and letting me go. What is he doing? I feel myself tense, and my vision swims, and he stops moving his hips. I cry out angrily, lifting my head and meeting him with a confused, desperate gaze.

"Hendrix, please . . ."

His eyes scan my face, and his expression is that of tortured pleasure. "Need to hear you beg, *inocencia*. Beg me . . ."

"Please," I whisper.

"More."

"Please, Hendrix, fuck me."

"More, sweetheart."

"Make me come. Be my first. Please, I want it so badly. Fuck me, make me never forget how this feels."

He growls, and he moves, sliding his cock up deep inside me once more. I whimper at the feeling of the sensitive nerves jumping back to life. He presses his thumb on my clit, and then begins rocking his hips again. The pleasure is back in a second, scorching through me like fire. I scream out his name, and thrust my hips down toward his deep plunging, wanting more, wanting it deeper. He growls, and lifts his hand off the wall beside me before tangling it into my hair and tugging it roughly.

I scream.

"You like that, don't you?" he groans.

"Oh. Yes. More."

He tugs my hair again, tilting it to the side so his teeth can find my neck. He begins nipping it softly, but his nipping becomes a gentle biting as his thrusts become more desperate. Oh, he's a biter. Oh. God. Yes. His teeth pinch at my flesh over and over, and his tongue swirls over the skin, while his hips buck, and his finger presses into my clit. The sensation is too much, and I finally tip over that edge. I feel the first surge of orgasm travel through my body, and I can hear my desperate scream as I relish in a pleasure I've never felt before.

"Fuck, I'm going to come," he roars, before biting my neck again as his entire body jerks, and I feel him pulsing inside me.

Each clench of my pussy around his cock has us both expressing our pleasure vocally. He groans, I moan, and together we drag each last shudder from each other's body. When we stop shaking he slowly moves me down until he slides out of me. He pulls the condom off, ties it, and reaches down to grip his jeans. Without looking at me, he pulls them on.

"You got clothes, Indi?"

I nod when he turns to look at me, but my legs are still wobbling and I'm holding on to the wall, too scared to actually take a step. My entire lower half is tingling. He gives me a lazy half-smile. "Are you goin' to move anytime soon?"

"Shut up," I murmur.

"Can't believe no man has ever gotten into that sweet pussy and made you come that hard."

I flush, and look down at my feet. My only boyfriend was sweet for a little while, before he started bashing me. It's no wonder I haven't had a great time with sex. He was always rough, and awful. Hendrix grips my chin and lifts my head until our eyes meet. "The only man you've been with is the one that bashed you, isn't it?"

I stiffen up, and pull my head from his hands. "It doesn't matter. We're not here to discuss what I've done and what I haven't. It was once, remember? You made that clear. I need to go."

I turn and lean down, gripping my bra and panties and shoving them on angrily before turning and heading back through the waterfall to get out. I can't deal with this right now.

"Indi!" he yells, but I don't stop.

My entire body is spinning, my head is fuzzy, and I'm confused. I'm confused because I don't know what to feel right now. I have something deep down in my body that's tugging at everything inside. I hate that feeling. I don't want to accept it, or even acknowledge it. It burns.

It's against the rules.

You're never meant to fall for your captor.

CHAPTER THIRTEEN

What do you do with a drunken sailor?

I find Jess and get myself a clean pair of clothes, and then we all gather around to make some breakfast over a little fire and grill plate. Hendrix hasn't come back from the lake yet, and I really don't want to think about what he's doing. Is he regretting what we just did? I have this tingle between my thighs every time I move, like a little reminder that he's been there, and that we stepped over that line.

"Are you okay?"

I turn to see Eric sit beside me on the tiny log I'm sitting on. I nod, and give him a weak smile.

"I'm fine, just tired and feeling a little off."

"Are you sick from the cold last night?"

I shake my head, "No, probably just tired."

Concern washes over his features. "The cave is empty. You should go and have a sleep."

I contemplate it, and actually think it's not a bad idea.

"I might, after lunch."

He leans in close, so no one else can hear us. "How are things really?"

"They're fine, Eric. I'm surviving."

"Do you think he'll let you go?"

"I don't know, okay?" I hiss.

I'm tired of him questioning me like I'm busting my ass for nothing.

"Why is the prisoner uncuffed?"

We hear Hendrix's gruff voice, and look up to see him walking back. He's still shirtless, and I can't help but let my eyes travel down his body. His chest is so defined, his abs just perfectly toned, and that dip into his jeans, or the little "V," as some call it, has everything inside me clenching. I lift my eyes and see that he's watching me with a heated expression. Oh. God. Drake stands and walks over to Eric, cuffing him again.

"Where the hell am I going to run to?" Eric grunts.

"Beside the point," Hendrix growls. "Your friend and I have a deal."

I glare at him, but lose it quickly when he turns to give orders to GG. Oh. Shit. His back has a couple of red gashes that I know are from my fingernails. I also know that every single person sitting in this camp right now knows that it's from me. We're the only two who disappeared this morning. My cheeks flush and I turn my eyes away, only to see that Eric's gaze is on Hendrix's back. He turns to me, and his nostrils flare.

I stand quickly.

"I need to . . . I mean, I need to have a rest."

Jess stands as I do, and she follows me as I avoid all the amused gazes and rush into the small cave. As soon as we get in, I turn to her, panicking.

"You slept with him, didn't you?" she says in a hushed whisper.

I cover my face with my hands. "Oh God, Jess. I thought . . . I just thought . . ."

"I know what you thought," she says softly, walking over and taking hold of my shoulders. "I know."

"I'm a fool."

"No, you're just doing whatever you can to protect your life. That doesn't make you a fool."

I lift my eyes and meet her gaze. She gives me a small smile.

"What do I do? Everyone knows now. He did that on purpose; he wanted to flaunt it."

"Honey, it's a small group. They would have figured it out. I'm almost sure they all think it's already happened."

"I need a minute, or just . . . I need a break."

"Go onto the ship. If you want to rest you'll have more chance of it there."

"Really?" I whisper.

"Yeah. Come on, I'll take you."

She takes my hand and leads me out. When we pass the small group, I avoid eye contact.

"Where you going, *inocencia*?" Hendrix purrs.

Asshole.

"She's going to rest. She's tired and the ship is quieter," Jess snaps.

She doesn't let him answer; she just continues pulling me past him and out through the trees.

The ship is still sitting up on the sand, but it's not damaged, so it's safe. We both head to the ladders and climb them. When we get on deck, I stare around. There are ropes and chains and all sorts of bits from the deck scattered everywhere. I guess that's why it takes them a day to tidy it back up. Plus, they would have to go over it for damage, which isn't a small process.

"I have to get some more clothes, but are you okay to rest, or do you want me to stay?" Jess says when we get into the hall.

I shake my head, giving her a weak smile. "I'm okay. I just need some sleep."

"Okay, well come and talk to me when you wake, all right? We'll have a chat."

I nod, and pull her in for a hug, "Thanks, Jess."

"It'll be okay," she says gently.

I feel my eyes burn with tears. "I'm not so sure it will. I'm terrified, Jess. I just . . ." My voice crackles. "I just want to go home."

Her eyes go glassy, and she hugs me closer. "It's going to be okay. We'll figure this out."

Then she steps back and smiles at me once more before disappearing down the halls. I head down until I reach Hendrix's room. I walk in and stare at my spot on the sofa with need. I'm exhausted, and I need a break. I walk over and drop down onto the sofa, tucking my legs up and sighing loudly. I can't remove the images of Hendrix having sex with me from my mind; they're haunting me in the most beautiful way. I'm not even sure I want to stop thinking about them.

I lie down, slowly letting my body sink into the soft sofa. I stare up at the roof, and my mind just spins. I have so many thoughts and feelings flying around that I can't pinpoint one long enough to process it. I hear the door creak, and I lift my head and see Hendrix stepping in. He shuts the door behind him and locks it. Oh crap. I sit up, and our eyes connect the entire time as he walks over and stops in front of me. Why is he in here? I made it clear that I wanted a break, that I needed to think, so why is he here staring down at me, like he wants to eat me alive?

"Stand up, *inocencia*," he husks.

"What? I . . . no . . ."

"Now," he orders firmly, yet his voice still holds that level of raw, sexual desire.

Like I have no control over my body, I stand slowly, my entire body trembling with . . . is that lust? Or something more? When I'm on my feet, Hendrix grips my arms and walks me out into the middle of the room. He stops me, and then turns and walks over to the sofa. What the hell? He sits down, leans back and puts his arms up behind his head, causing those muscles to flex and pull. I watch him in confusion.

"I wasn't done, earlier. I said once, but I didn't mean that I would put my cock in you once; I meant that I would have one session with you. I'm not finished with that session. Now, get your clothes off."

My mouth drops open, and I feel my fingers fumbling nervously together. "I . . . I . . ."

"*Inocencia,*" he rasps. "Now, baby."

My entire body is on fire, and I don't want to deny him. The thought of having him buried deep inside me again is removing every other logical thought from my mind, and replacing it with a deep, intense need that is so strong I can't fight it. I grip my shirt and go to lift it but he puts a hand up, stopping me. He gets to his feet, walks over to his desk, and presses a few buttons on a small set of speakers. A moment later, a familiar song comes on. I watch as he turns and then walks back over and sits down, resuming his position.

"Take them off, slowly," he growls.

He wants me to . . . strip? I hear the song flare to life, and my cheeks flush. Well, it *is* a stripper song. The words "She's my cherry pie" fill the room, and it takes everything inside me not to flick my hair around and dance like a wild girl. This song just does that to me. Instead, I grip my shirt again and slowly begin swaying my hips from side to side. I've not ever undressed like this in front of a man before, and the idea of it is completely erotic. My entire body is tingling with shame, yet I can't stop.

When I meet Hendrix's lusty gaze, it only spurs me on.

It could be a great chance for me to make him want me so desperately he can't look back.

At least that's what I'm telling myself.

I continue swaying my hips while my fingers slowly lift the top. When I reach my breasts, I flick my head and do a half-curve of my body, making my hair flick and my body twist in an extremely sexual manner. I lift myself back up, wiggling my hips as I lift the shirt over my head. When I gaze at Hendrix, he's so damned hard his jeans are straining against his cock. His fists are clenched and his eyes are wild with need.

"Keep going," he rasps.

I toss my shirt onto the ground, and I spin around so my back is facing him. I wrap my arms around myself and wiggle my ass as I unclip my bra. I shimmy it off and toss it onto the ground. I hear Hendrix suck in a breath, and my cheeks flush even more. I slide my hands down my body, still swaying my hips gently, and I grip my shorts. Doing my best "ass girl" maneuver, I slowly grip them and move my hands down my body with them, leaving my ass in the air. Hendrix growls, and I know that he's enjoying the view.

I step out of my shorts and slowly run my hands back up my body before looking over my shoulder at him. His fingers are pressing into his thighs, and he's breathing deeply. God, he looks so fucking yummy, sitting there, looking so desperate. He lifts his hand and twirls his fingers. "Spin, baby. Let me see."

I do as he asks, and slowly turn. I see his entire body go rigid when I am facing him, and my heart begins to pound. My fingers are up near my breasts, semi-covering them. "Drop the hands, *inocencia*," he rasps.

Slowly, I lower my hands. His eyes widen, and he makes a deep throaty groaning sound.

"Dance, baby. I need you to dance. Move."

I begin to sway my hips again, and slowly I let my fingers slide over my body. I close my eyes, taking myself to another place. Knowing his eyes are on me—God, it's a feeling I can't quite describe. He's making everything inside me come alive, but most of all, he's making me feel . . . beautiful, sexy, alluring . . . hell, he's making me feel like a woman. I've never felt that in all my life.

"Eyes on me, sweetheart," he hisses.

I open my eyes and meet his. And we hold that look as I slowly move my fingers down and hook them into my panties. I begin swaying my hips and lowering myself again, only this time I keep my eyes on his. His gaze doesn't stray; he doesn't let his eyes move from mine. He just watches me, letting those deep brown eyes burn into me. I step out of my panties as soon as they're lowered, and then, slowly, I move up, until I'm standing. Heat flares in my cheeks, and I break eye contact with Hendrix.

"Are you ashamed?" he murmurs, moving so he's standing. Then he stalks toward me.

"No, I . . ."

"You're fucking exquisite, *inocencia*. Like a fucking dream."

His words make my entire body break out in shivers. I wrap my arms around myself, at which he reaches out and stops me. His fingers curl around my wrists, and he pulls them up above my head, raising my breasts. His gaze lowers, and his jaw flexes as he watches my nipples harden beneath his gaze. Slowly, he lowers his head, still holding my arms up, and he captures my nipple in his mouth. I gasp, and my legs wobble as he begins to swirl his tongue around and around, causing a pathetic little whimper to escape from my lips.

When he closes his teeth over it, and a little pinch shoots through my chest, my knees do buckle.

He gently lowers me onto the floor, and his hard body falls over mine. I can feel his erection pressing between my legs as I widen them to accommodate him. His jeans press right to my core, and when I shift, he hisses. "You're so fucking hot, I can feel it through my jeans. Fuck, *inocencia*, I need to be inside you again."

I whimper and drop my head onto the floor as his lips find my neck. The desperate need to taste him is beyond anything I've ever felt. I want his lips on mine, I want his tongue to dance with mine—I just want to see what he tastes like. I need to know what he tastes like, more than anything, I am desperate to crush my lips against his. Feeling them sliding up my neck to nip at my ear makes that need so much more intense. How can one man be so incredibly addictive?

"On the couch I want you to ride me, but first, I want your sweet mouth around my cock," he murmurs into my ear, before wrapping his arms around me and lifting us both.

He turns us and walks over to the sofa, sitting himself down and pulling me over him. I'm straddling him; our bodies are rubbing together and our faces are close. Slowly, without thinking, I move my lips in closer. Before I can make it, his hand slides up and tangles in my hair, halting me. We're so close that I can feel his warm breath tickling my lips. Our eyes are locked, and the heat sizzling between us is so intense my entire body is on alert.

"You know the rules," he murmurs. "No kissing."

I bite my lower lip, and let my eyes travel down to his lips. So full, so manly, and I long to feel that stubble rubbing against my lips as I slide them all over him.

"What about other places?" I whisper, lifting my eyes.

"You can kiss me anywhere else," he rasps.

I move my head in closer, tilting it to the side and pressing it just outside of the corner of his mouth. He releases my hair, and makes a pained growling sound. I slide my tongue out, making a small circle, before moving across his jaw. I can taste him; the faint saltiness to his skin is actually quite a turn-on. The small spikes of stubble that my tongue encounters every now and then just spark me on. When I reach his ear, I slide my tongue out and flick his earlobe. He curses, and his hands slide between my legs, pushing them apart so I'm straddling him fully, and then his fingers slide in to find my damp clit.

I groan and lift my hand, cupping the other side of his face as I move my lips over his cheek. He drops his head back, eyes closed, fingers still sliding along my pussy. He likes it, and he's letting me be this close to him, even if it's just for a moment. I slide my mouth up, kissing his skin, and then I pepper little kisses over his eyelids before moving down his nose and pressing one to the end. He groans as I move my lips down past his lips and give his chin a gentle suck.

"Shit, *inocencia*, I need to fuck you."

I drop my head and find his neck. I trail kisses down, stopping every now and then to give him a gentle suck. His fingers find my entrance, and he thrusts them inside me. I mewl and rotate my hips to feel more of him. I lower my mouth to his collarbone, and here I can smell him the strongest. He's got a musky, very masculine scent. I nip at his skin before sliding my mouth over his shoulders. He fucks me with his fingers so skillfully, tilting them at that perfect angle, that he has me coming in a matter of minutes. I push myself closer to him, burying my face into his shoulder as I shudder, feeling little jerks of pleasure traveling from my pussy right up my spine.

"Now, baby," he breathes. "Suck me."

Oh.

Yes.

I slowly slide off his lap, and as I move, he grips his jeans and undoes them, jerking them down just enough to free his cock. When I am on my knees in front of him, elbows resting on his thighs, I take a moment to gaze at the large, extremely erotic sight before me. He has a beautiful cock, so thick, so long, so perfectly shaped. I reach out, wrapping my fingers around it, and then, slowly, I lower my head. I slide my tongue out first, letting it swirl around the tip. He hisses and his hips jerk upward.

"Don't tease, *inocencia*," he groans.

I press him against my cheek, feeling the hot, smooth skin there. Then I turn my head and I lower my mouth onto him. He growls so loudly I pause, actually wondering if I've hurt him. "Don't stop," he pants.

Spurred on, I lower my mouth farther, sucking and swirling my tongue as I go. When I've taken him as deep as I can I begin gently lifting my head, and then repeating this over and over until I've got a gentle yet firm bobbing motion happening. Hendrix's hands tangle in my hair, and he jerks his hips, hissing my name as I begin to move faster, using my hand to pump the base of his cock while my mouth deals with the rest.

"Shit, fuck, stop," he growls suddenly, gripping my shoulders and pulling me back.

He tugs me upward, and as I move he takes a condom from his jeans and tears it open, then he fumbles almost desperately to get it out of the packet. His entire chest is straining, his muscles bunching and releasing. It's beyond hot. I watch as he rolls the condom over his cock, which is red and angry, like it's about to explode. He grips me, pulling me forward. I don't get the chance to have a moment to think because he's pressing a hand to the small of my back and sinking me down onto him before I can even speak.

I don't need to speak.

All that comes out of my mouth as he slowly fills me is a ragged moan. My pussy stretches around him, and the feeling is so intense I feel my head begin to spin. I close my eyes and drop my head back.

"Eyes, *inocencia*," he rasps, gripping my chin and turning my face back toward his. I open my eyes and once again, we lock in that moment that's just ours. Nothing else comes through; it's as though no one else exists when he's looking at me like that.

"Won't last long," he murmurs. "Too fucking sweet."

He grips my hip, and begins grinding me against him, stopping the up and down motion that I had just begun to create. The grinding is better, though, oh, it is better. He makes small circular movements that have his cock pressing against my inner walls, finding that sweet spot. I whimper and begin taking over the action on my own. The deep grinding continues and his hands move up and cup my breasts, his thumbs making little circles over my nipples.

"Hendrix," I rasp. "I . . . oh, God . . ."

"Come for me, *inocencia*. Scream my name."

I jerk, and when his finger slides down to find my clit, I come. It's better than in the waterfall earlier—different, but definitely better. This time, I scream so loud my throat closes off, causing my scream to end in a choking gasp.

"H . . . Hendrix," I stammer, still clenching and shuddering over him.

"Going to come, oh, fuck, now," he roars, and then he jerks his hips up suddenly, and I can feel him pulsing as I clench, and our cries of pleasure mix together to make the most beautiful sound.

I slump against him, my head dropping onto his chest. A fine sheen of sweat covers his skin, and I find myself sliding my tongue out to have a taste. Oh, yes. Hendrix takes my face, lifting it off his chest.

"Enough, *inocencia*, or I'll fuck you again."

Well maybe I want him to.

I pull my chin away from him, and put my head back on his chest, exhaling loudly. He surprises me by putting an arm around my waist and resting it there, but to me, it feels as though he's holding me. It's a nice feeling.

"Tell me about your life," he murmurs softly above me.

"My life?" I say in a small exhausted voice.

"Yeah, your life."

I nestle further into him, truly feeling this moment with him. "I'm not sure it really matters in the big scheme of things, does it?"

"No," he murmurs. "I suppose not. Tell me anyway."

Wanting to extend this moment together, maybe make a bit more of a connection, I decide to talk to him.

"Well, you know about Kane..."

"That his name?" he grunts, and I feel it rumble through my cheek. "Kane?"

"Yeah, that's his name."

"You met him how?"

"I met him in foster care. We were foster brother and sister in a home, so to speak. We grew close, and we moved out and away together as soon as I was old enough. Things were great for a long time, until I started seeing his violent side. The beatings started, and they just didn't stop. I got so tired of them, so emotionally damaged, that I ended up fearing for my life. That night he beat me... I had to protect myself. I was hiding in a cupboard when he found me, and we wrestled for a long time with the gun. He had it pointed to my face so many times I was sure my life would end, but I managed to be the one to get the shot in. I injured him badly, he went to jail, and just before I went on the yacht he got released. I knew I had to start my life again, so I decided to leave the country. The night before I left he contacted me, threatening me, and I knew I had to go."

"Fucker wouldn't want to cross paths with me. I'd kill him."

I snort. "He wouldn't find me now."

"Damn right he won't. Did you get charged?"

"No, I was acting in self-defense. But the investigation was quite draining."

We're silent a minute, and he begins drawing small circles on my back.

"What about your parents?"

"I had a good life, and then my dad started running off the rails and disappearing. I mentioned earlier that he left. Well, it was true. One night he went, and never came back. My mom died—she was ill with cancer—and after that I just got sent off."

"So you assume your dad's still alive, then?"

"I think he is . . . he just disappeared. How can one person just disappear? It never made sense. Sometimes I hoped he was dead, because it made it easier to process the pain of why he didn't come back."

"You ever tried to find him?" he asks, shifting, and wrapping his arms around me tighter.

It's nice.

"No, I don't have enough resources. Money isn't an issue. It's finding people who are willing to help."

"What's his name? I might be able to help."

My heart hammers. He might be able to help? As in, he might reconsider selling me? Everything inside me floods with warmth.

"Charles Waters."

Hendrix jerks as though he's been hit. "What did you say?"

"I . . . that's my father's name."

Suddenly I'm being tossed off him, as if I'm no more than a rag doll. He slides from my body quickly, leaving it feeling odd for a moment. He gets to his feet, yanks his jeans up, and storms over to his desk, shoving through papers. What the hell is happening?

"Do you know him? Will you help me find him? Will you reconsider selling me?" I babble before I can stop myself. His frantic behavior has me wondering if he knows my father, and hope swells in my chest.

He spins around, his eyes filled with something I can't understand . . . Fear? Rage? He storms over, gripping my shoulder. "You're not staying here, so stop fucking thinking all this is going to change that."

Then he turns and practically runs out the door.

What the hell just happened?

My heart drops into my stomach, and everything hurts.

Back to square one.

CHAPTER FOURTEEN

Landlubber!

I clean up before heading out of the ship. It's late afternoon, and the sun has finally come out, so I walk a long way down the beach, not wanting to go to the camp, and I find myself a spot on the slowly drying sand to sit down. It sticks to my legs, and my foot, I realize, is aching, but I don't care. I'm confused. Hendrix and I, we had a moment, and then he just ran out. His words hurt. All along, I thought maybe we were creating something, but all along he was just fucking me. There's nothing more to it. Maybe the idea that he actually considered helping me hit home, and he realized he was getting too close.

I try to push thoughts of Hendrix from my mind and instead focus on the beautiful sun. I am grateful that Hendrix decided to allow us a few days on the island as an escape from the ship. The sunshine, land, and fresh air are something I've been desperately missing. It also gives me space, which is also something I've lacked since I've been here. I've enjoyed finding quiet spots to myself to just think and take some time out.

"I've been looking for you."

I hear Jess's voice, and I look up to see her standing there, smiling down at me. "Hendrix said he couldn't find you . . ."

I turn away, and swallow. I won't cry. I won't show that kind of weakness. I have held myself together so well that to fail now would break me. Jess sits down beside me and puts an arm around my shoulders.

"He was . . . behaving oddly. Barking orders, and talking closely with Drake. He seemed panicked, and then he couldn't find you, and he exploded. I told him I'd come and see where you were."

She rubs my shoulders and pulls me in close to her side.

"We had a moment, and then there was a second when I thought I had a chance of escape and freedom, but he turned it around. He's not going to change his mind about selling me. I don't want to be sold. I don't want this to be how my life goes."

"I'm going to help you," she whispers. "I won't let him sell you, Indi."

I lift my head, meeting her gaze. "What?"

"You're not getting sold . . ."

"There's no escape, Jess, you know that. I've tried. I can't get Eric and escape without being noticed. I can't do both . . ."

"Yes, you can."

I shake my head. "I don't understand."

She swallows, and turns and stares behind us. When she turns back to me, I see she's worried. About what I'm not sure, but I bet I'm about to find out.

"What's going on, Jess?"

"Eric will be here in about an hour. Hendrix put him back in his cell; I'm not really sure why. I convinced Hendrix I'm taking him to see you and that you won't like the idea that he has put Eric back in the cell. He felt for you, so he let me."

"What? Why?"

"I called the sea police, Indigo."

My eyes widen. "I don't . . . I don't understand."

"I can't let him do this to you, and the longer you're out on that ocean, the less chance you have of escaping."

"But . . . how . . ."

She leans in close. "I told him this afternoon that we needed some more medical supplies. With the storm season upon us, he didn't even think twice about it. He trusts me. He knows I have no reason to betray him . . . so when he handed me the phone and walked out, I made the call. I knew where we were: I made a point of listening to the coordinates of this island when they were talking . . ."

"Jess," I gasp. "That's dangerous . . ."

"It's the only way. He's never going to dock with you on the ship—he is too worried you will escape. I overheard him talking, and the swap will be done out at sea. You can't possibly escape out in that ocean. There's nowhere to run to."

"Hendrix will kill them, Jess. You know he will."

"It's worth the risk."

"What if they kill Hendrix?" I whisper.

Her face tightens. "I told them to come to the north of the island. I'll make sure you and Eric are at opposite ends to the pirates. If for some reason he figures it out, you should be too far gone by the time they get to this side."

I feel my heart begin to thump. "Jess, if he finds out it was you . . ."

She grips my hand, squeezing it hard. "I can't let you be sold, honey."

I tremble and rub my arms. Is this it? Is this really going to be my freedom? I repeat Hendrix's words in my head, and I know that my attempts at making him change his mind are just that: attempts. I am the only one with growing feelings; he made it clear that he has none. If I stay, it will only hurt more when the moment comes for me to leave him. It will break me, and I can't live with that.

I turn to Jess. "Come with me," I plead, gripping her hands.

"You know I can't. My life is here. I have nothing but a life of running on the land."

She looks sad, her green eyes empty. She really has no way out.

"You don't want it to be here, though, do you?"

She looks away. "What I want and what I have are two different things, but it doesn't mean I'm not grateful."

"Well, you're a better woman than me."

"Jess?"

I stiffen when I hear the sound of Hendrix's voice coming up from behind us. We both turn, and see Hendrix, fully clothed now, standing and staring down at us. Jess turns to me and mouths "one hour," and then she stands. She's risking her life for me. I don't know why, but I know I'll be forever grateful to her for it. When she disappears into the trees, Hendrix walks over and then drops down beside me. He's got a first aid kit in his hands. It's clear he didn't hear us, as he's acting far too casual.

"You need to clean your foot."

I stare out at the ocean. The water is clearing now; that soft haze is disappearing and showing the aqua water that is just stunning.

"Indi?"

I turn and meet Hendrix's gaze. "Why are you here?"

He shakes his head in confusion. "To clean your foot."

"Why? We both know I'm no more than a sale to you. So stop pretending my life actually matters."

He growls and takes my foot, tugging it toward him. I lost the shirt he wrapped around it last night, and I can see the deep gash in my foot now. It's kind of dirty, and I'm ashamed that I didn't clean it up sooner. No, instead I let Hendrix seduce me . . . again. I was never in control. *Never*. Hendrix opens the kit and begins cleaning up my foot. A sharp sting shoots up my leg, and I grit my teeth to stop from crying out.

"I'm not going to let you sit in pain."

I shake my head. "What?"

"You think you're no more than a sale, but I'm not going to let you suffer."

"Did that truly mean nothing to you before?" I whisper. "Is it really that easy to just fuck someone and walk away?"

He stiffens, and he lifts his gaze to mine. "I told you what I am, Indi. When did you get that confused?"

"And I'm asking if what we felt was a lie?" I scream suddenly, feeling my hands shake.

He puts a bandage on my foot, and drops it. I need to know. If I'm about to run, and never see him again, I need to know. I have to hear his answer, because a big part of me is hoping he will say it meant something and he doesn't want to sell me, because a tiny part of me wants to stay here with him, and I don't understand it. I need a reason to go . . . I just can't do it on my own.

"It's beside the point."

"Just answer me one thing then," I snarl, getting to my feet. "Are you even reconsidering selling me after that? Was there even a goddamned moment where you thought about changing your mind?"

He stiffens, and his eyes search my face. "Don't go there, Indigo."

"Just answer me, goddammit. Fucking answer me, you gutless pig! The least you can fucking do is give it to me straight."

"No," he bellows. "I am not reconsidering selling you, because you're nothing more to me than a moment of fun."

My entire face drains of blood, and my knees wobble. Everything in my world spins. He . . . he feels nothing. Nothing at all. I've been living in a fantasy. I've been fooling myself, thinking that he would ever see me as anything more than a debt payment. My entire body is shaking, to the point where my teeth are clattering together. I open my mouth, but nothing comes out. Nothing but a rasping hiss. I turn slowly, feeling like I'm going to collapse at any second.

He doesn't stop me.

I'm sure that hurts more.

Why is it that we, as humans, always hope that something will change, even when we know the answer? We're walking away, broken, ripped to pieces, and yet we're still hoping that something will happen to make it all go away. Fact is, nothing can take away the harsh pain of cruel words. *Nothing.* I hobble down the beach, and I let the tears flow. I was a fool, and that's on me.

I get to the north end of the island where Jess told me Eric would be, and I collapse against a tree. My head spins, and my body aches. It throbs in the worst way, and in the best. I can smell Hendrix on me—I can feel the ache between my legs that equally matches the ache in my heart. It's a pain I'm almost sure I'll never forget. A mix of betrayal, and desperation, and something else I can't name, or maybe I'm just too scared to face it.

I hear the sound of rustling leaves, and I turn to see Eric and Jess appear. Right now, I'm as grateful as anyone can be for Jess. She's saving my life, even if she doesn't know it. Eric sees me. His face softens and he walks over, pulling me into his arms.

I let him, because I need him.

Jess grips my hand, and I press my cheek to Eric's chest. He's gotten skinnier; I can feel the bones in his chest pressing into my face. He pulls back and stares down at me, stroking a piece of hair from my face.

"We're going home. It's all going to be over soon."

"I am only guessing the time, but they should be here in a bit," Jess says, scanning the horizon.

"I can't thank you enough for this, Jess," I rasp.

She takes me from Eric's arms and holds me tight. "I see something in you, and I can't let you be given to a rogue pirate because of a debt Hendrix created for himself."

"He told me I mean nothing," I whisper, trembling.

"I don't believe him, but I'm also not willing to put my money on it. You need your freedom back. I never got a choice, and I'll regret that forever, but you have a choice, Indi. I couldn't just sit back and let that be taken from you, knowing that you had a chance at escape..."

Tears burn under my eyelids as I squeeze her close. "I'll be forever grateful."

We all sit in silence for about twenty minutes. What is there to say? We're all thinking different things, and we're all terrified.

"Ladies... is that... a ship?" Eric says suddenly.

We both lift our heads to see a small ship in the distance moving closer to the island. My heart thumps, and I get to my feet. This is it. I shove any thoughts of Hendrix from my head. I have to. I can't... I just can't... I have to protect myself and my friend. Hendrix will fade; he'll fade. I tell myself this, over and over, as we walk toward the ocean. Jess lifts her hands, and she does some sort of signal. The small ship nears us.

"They won't be able to stop. You're going to have to swim out," she says.

"B... b... but..."

"It's the only way," she says frantically.

"We're going to be okay," Eric says, grabbing my hand and tugging me toward the water.

I turn, tears tumbling down my cheeks. I hold out my arms and Jess comes to me, wrapping me in a hug. "I'll never forget this, Jess, never."

"Be safe, and find the life you deserve."

I hug her harder, and then let her go, taking Eric's hand. He squeezes it tight, and we take our first step into the water, our first step to freedom. The cool water washes up my leg, and I tremble. My entire body is prickling, my heart is pounding, and my head is spinning. Adrenalin fills my veins. One moment, it's all we need, and yet anything could change it so easily.

When we're waist deep and the ship is in clear view, my heart begins to speed up, until I can hardly breathe through the pounding.

I can see the men in white suits standing, waving us closer. Freedom. It's so close. This is what I've been fighting for since I got captured, so why the hell does it feel so damned wrong? Why is my heart aching? Why am I struggling to breathe?

We begin swimming, no longer able to walk, and that's when everything changes. The man closest to us, who is standing, leaning over and encouraging us forward, suddenly jerks, and blood splatters from his head as he slides forward and drops into the water. A strangled scream escapes my throat, and my legs turn to jelly. I struggle to keep swimming as I turn my eyes to the shore. I see Hendrix, holding up a gun. He has Drake beside him, who is also holding a gun.

Another shot rings out.

Another man drops.

Blood fills the ocean, swirling and surrounding us, and the bodies slowly begin sinking, lives wasted. Oh, God. Eric grips me, forcing me forward, kicking with all his might.

"Keep swimming, Indi!"

"Th-th-they're dead," I wail.

"Get back here, Indigo, or I keep killing them. You're mine, goddammit, don't make me force you back!" Hendrix roars, and it sounds like a far-off hum.

"Don't listen to him, Indi! Keep swimming."

Another shot is fired, from the ship this time. I turn my head frantically, but see that everyone on the shore is still standing.

"Fuck it, Indi, get back here. You're mine!" Hendrix bellows.

You're mine.

He doesn't mean that.

He doesn't.

"Don't you listen," Eric cries, tugging me closer.

We're swimming hard, and the ship is getting closer and closer. Men are lining the outside, guns pointed. Another shot rings out, and another one drops into the water. I wail loudly, and saltwater fills my mouth and I begin to choke. He's putting this on me, and I know that if I don't stop swimming, he will keep killing. I cough and splutter, and my legs are aching so badly that each movement is painful. I begin to struggle in the water, my mind making me doubt my actions.

"Don't let him do this. He's the one with the gun, he's the one killing them," Eric yells, not letting me go.

"I . . . I . . . I have to go back. I can't let him kill any more."

"You keep swimming, goddammit!" he screams, pulling me.

"Eric, please!"

"No, we're not going back."

"Keep swimming," one of the men yells. "You're nearly here."

My vision blurs, and I'm hiccupping and crying so loudly I sound like a wounded animal. Eric is pulling, guns are shooting, Hendrix is screaming, and I'm hyperventilating. The next few minutes pass as a blur. We wade past at least six sinking bodies, and the water is filled with a reddish color that is fading to almost brown. By the time we reach the ship, I'm completely out of it. Eric is holding my weight, because I have nothing left.

I hear the sound of more gunshots.

I feel them pull me up.

And then everything goes black.

∽

"Hey, Indi, wake up."

My eyelids flutter open, and I see Eric's face. The moment I realize where I am, and what has happened, a sick feeling crashes into my chest, and my stomach turns. I roll off the bed, crying out in pain as I lean over the side and throw up. All those people. *Dead*. Because of me. It was hard enough knowing John the yacht owner died because I didn't fight hard enough to convince Eric to let me save him. But now this? The one thing I knew I could never recover from was being the reason someone died. I throw up until I'm dry-heaving and gasping for air.

"Oh, Indi," Eric soothes, stroking my hair.

"It's all my fault," I sob.

"No, it's not. He did it. He was the one who made the decision to shoot them."

"If I had just gone back . . ."

"Indi, he would have shot them anyway. He's a goddamned pirate. Do you honestly believe he's never done anything like that in his life?"

"Stop!" I cry, covering my face.

"We're free, we're going to get home and . . ."

"And what?" I scream. "And live in fear? Live our lives running? What, Eric?"

"We're going to be okay."

Black and white. Black and fucking white. He sees nothing else.

"Indigo?"

I lift my head to see a tall, dark-haired man coming into the room. He's wearing a crisp white sailor suit. He has kind blue eyes.

"That's me," I whisper, sitting up.

"Are you ill?"

"No."

He nods, and walks in farther. "I'll have someone look after that mess for you. If you have a minute, I'd like to talk to you about our plans."

"Plans?" I rasp.

"Obviously you're not safe until we get you out of the ship and onto a plane home, but before then we're going to need some statements. Now, you're safe here with us, but when we arrive at the small docking island we're going to have to keep full cover on you until we can sort out safe transportation. Even after you arrive home, I would suggest full watch for a few months at least."

"W . . . w . . . w . . . we're stopping at an island?"

"It's a small town, really. We have full protection for you there, but you will need to follow instructions. We're not sure what we're dealing with yet, and whether or not you're in danger."

"They're pirates," I snap. "Of course I'm in danger."

"Pirates, you say?"

"Look, I'm not doing this, okay? I'm not giving you all this information, because you're unable to do anything to stop them. I won't go there, because there's no point. They've been out there for over ten years—nothing you do will change that. I just want to go home and forget this ever happened."

"Indi," Eric snarls. "You need to give a statement against him."

"Why, Eric?" I yell. "What is going to change?"

"He needs to pay."

"He's not going to pay. You know that as well as I do, and so does he," I snap, pointing to the officer.

"We have our ways, so we need a full statement to ensure your safety. When we arrive at the island we will check you into a hotel, and keep you there with watch until we can figure out the safest mode of transportation home."

"Whatever," I whisper, lying down and rolling over. "Can you just leave me be?"

"If you need anything, don't hesitate to ask," the officer says, before leaving the room.

I feel Eric shift beside me. "Why are you protecting him?"

"I'm not protecting him, Eric," I whisper. "I'm simply stating facts."

"He was going to sell you, and you're basically refusing to give information."

"He's a goddamned pirate," I snarl, spinning and glaring at him. "He's not getting anything done to him because he IS the fucking law on the ocean."

Eric's face shifts, and he lifts a hand and runs it through his hair. "You care about him, don't you?"

"No!"

"Oh . . . my . . . God," he rasps. "You fucking care about the mongrel bastard who was going to sell you! What the hell is wrong with you, Indi?"

"Don't, Eric."

"Don't?" he screams. "Don't what? Tell you how stupid you are? What the hell possessed you to be so stupid? What could he have possibly done to make you feel anything more than hatred for him?"

"It was probably how he fucked me," I snarl.

My hands are trembling, and deep down I'm horrified by my words, but right now I have no emotions. I'm just numb.

Eric reels backward and clasps a hand over his chest. "I knew it!"

"Yeah," I bark. "I'm sure you did, and you should know, Eric. It was amazing."

Eric slaps me. His hand lashes out and connects with my face. I yelp and fall backward, gripping my face in horror.

"I sat rotting in a fucking cell, and you were off screwing the man who put us in that position?"

"I was trying to save your fucking life!" I scream. "I was doing whatever it took to get us out of there."

"Only you wanted to fucking do it, so it doesn't make it a good thing," he spits.

"Get out," I rasp. "Get the hell out."

"With pleasure," he barks, before turning and storming out of the room.

The door slams, and I fall back onto my bed with a broken sob. God help me.

Nothing in my life has ever felt worse than how I feel right now.

CHAPTER FIFTEEN

Avast there!

I don't move from that bed until we stop, not for anything. We dock at the town on the small island, and I simply follow instructions. Eric doesn't speak to me as they move us off the ship and onto the dry land. My legs wobble as I follow the officers, two on either side of me, into town. Eric is behind me; he's also under full protection until they can get us home. The idea of going home isn't as thrilling as I thought it would be. It just feels . . . empty. Like my life will just never be the same again.

"We will settle you into a hotel room each, letting you get some rest until we can figure out the safest method to get you off the island," the dark-haired officer from the other night says.

I don't answer him. Eric doesn't either.

I just walk.

I do peer around at the small town. It's old. It looks as though it was built in the early 1900s. The houses and shops are all wooden and showing signs of disarray. The few roads that travel through the roads are crappy and need serious work. There are a lot of older people walking around, and to the left is a massive wharf with hundreds of yachts and ships. I guess its main purpose is for people to dock. I can see a few large warehouses that I would assume are full of supplies.

We walk down a few streets until we reach a motel. It's old, with faded yellow paint and trees that have seen better days. It's privacy, though, and I need that. The dark-haired officer walks us into the reception area, where we are greeted by a red-haired lady with glasses. "Hello, how may I help you?"

"I rang earlier. My name is Lyle."

Lyle.

The red-haired lady turns her eyes to us, and they widen. What? Did Lyle tell her who we are? Does she know we are the people who went missing? How many people know?

"Of course. I have two rooms ready."

"And where can my officers stand that won't cause a problem for other guests?"

"Anywhere. It's not a problem."

"Thank you," Lyle says, taking two sets of keys from her.

Like two zombies, Eric and I turn and follow him out. We walk down an old crappy cement path until we meet two doors, both old, brown, and faded. Lyle unlocks the first one and turns to me. "This is you, Indigo."

I step into the room and wrinkle my nose. It's not very . . . appealing. There's an old double bed in the middle of the room. To the left are an office desk and a crappy plastic chair. I can't see the bathroom, but I guess it's through the door to the right of the bed. There's a small drinks fridge and a microwave, plus a torn leather couch and a tiny box television.

"I know it's not very nice, but we're hoping it's only for a night. Room service is available twenty-four hours. It's on us, so order what you like."

I nod, and turn to him. "Thanks," I croak.

"We will have a guard at every entrance of the complex for your protection, and here's my number if you're ever worried or frightened."

He hands me a card. I take it and stare up at him. "I don't have a phone."

"There's one in the room. You can use that any time."

I nod and wrap my arms around myself. "Is that all?"

"Yes," he says, giving me a half-assed smile before turning and exiting the room.

When he's gone, I walk over to the bed and drop down, wrapping my arms around myself.

I feel empty.

I feel numb.

And I don't understand it.

∼

I lock my door and don't communicate with anyone for the rest of the night. I go to bed early, and my exhausted body falls into a deep sleep. When I wake in the morning, I don't feel any better. Everything inside me still aches. I miss him, and it makes no sense to me. Nothing is comprehensible to me right now, and I hate that I'm longing for someone who has no feelings, who doesn't care about me or my life.

I have a shower and hop into a new set of clothes that was handed to me the night before, and then I order some breakfast before curling back up on the bed and flicking the television on. As soon as it flickers to life, Eric's and my faces are all over the screen. I sit up, and stare at it in shock. Our pictures are all over the news with labels like "Miracle survival after a yacht accident." I get off the bed and walk closer, listening to the report as a woman with mousy brown hair speaks into a microphone as if she knows what she's talking about.

She doesn't.

"Indigo Waters and Eric George were found late yesterday, after they went missing over a week ago. The two were on a yacht that sank after an accidental explosion. The waters were searched for a few days after, but there was no sign of survivors. It was said the captain of the yacht was taking a shortcut, and wasn't on a normal route. The two have been recovered safely, and are both well. More to come in an hour."

John was taking a shortcut? He took us into those waters? Is that what they're saying? I shake my head and rub my hands over my stomach, feeling off. Now the entire world knows, and yet they don't, really. They're so far from the truth. I get off the bed, and am just about to head to the phone to ask Lyle about the media having our photos when there's a knock on my door. With a weak sigh, I walk over and swing it open to see Eric. He's pale and trembling. Maybe he saw the news too?

"Eric, what's . . ."

Before I can finish my sentence, Kane steps into view. My entire world stops. I open my mouth and inhale with shock as I lay eyes on the man whom I was running from, and the man who somehow steered me here. He looks different, and yet so much the same. His eyes are still as cold and blue as they always were, and his once short blond hair is now long and whipping around his neck. To onlookers, Kane is an extremely attractive man. To me, he's a monster.

"K . . . K . . . Kane, I don't . . ."

"Hello, Indigo. Long time, no see."

He moves closer and raises a gun. My knees wobble, and I reach out and grasp the door, holding myself upright as fear shoots through my body.

"Well, aren't you going to invite me in?"

I step back, unable to do anything else. Eric meets my terrified stare, and he begins to tremble harder. Kane shoves him through the doorway, and then slams the door behind him before spinning to us both, pointing the gun in our direction.

"Sit. Now."

We both take the few steps back toward the bed, and slowly lower ourselves onto it. Kane begins to pace the room, tapping the gun into his palm.

"H . . . h . . . h . . . how did you get here?" I whisper.

He spins to me, and a low, throaty chuckle escapes his throat. "It was easy. The media had a story on you, and had been plastering your face over the news for the last week when the yacht that went down got reported in. Only one body was found, and the rescue boat was gone. I figured you would survive—either that or you were dead, but I wasn't risking the off chance that you would show up and I'd miss my chance to kill you like you deserve, so I flew over and started scouring these small islands."

"Then, yesterday, I saw your faces all over the news again. They'd found you, and you were safely on an island until you were to be flown home. There's only one island in this area, and I recognized the background of the interview with the reporter who spoke to the navy. I got on a plane and was here in less than two hours. I was out this morning, wondering about my next move, when Eric showed up in the store I was in. It was like everything I had ever planned was falling into place. I threatened him with a gun to his balls, and told him to pretend I was his brother and take me back to his room. Your idiot officer friends didn't even question him."

Oh.

God.

I try to get into survival mode, and think about all the things we were taught about removing oneself from a situation like this.

Keep them talking, don't make them angry, try and get help. I let my eyes flicker to the phone in the kitchenette. I just have to get to it . . . and call Lyle. I need a distraction first, though, something to take Kane's mind off me.

"Go right ahead and kill me, Kane. I couldn't care less," I mutter, in a monotone voice.

His face flickers with confusion before he makes a snorting sound. "Don't even try that one on, Indigo. I'm not letting you get away with it that easily. No, I'm going to make this hurt. I'm going to make you watch your friend here scream, then I'm going to kill you slowly, painfully, while you relive every moment you put me through fucking hell."

"You deserved it!" I spit.

So much for keeping him calm.

He storms over, and he hits my cheek so hard with the butt of his gun that my head spins. I topple backwards, and I whimper in agony as I feel a strong, intense ache begin pulsing in my cheek and moving through my head. That's going to bruise.

"Get up," Kane bellows.

"Please stop," Eric cries.

"Shut the fuck up, Nancy boy, or I'll cut your dick off and shove it down your throat."

Eric makes a whimpering sound, and Kane grips me, hurling me up. I cry out and land on the floor in front of him with a thump. My knees scrape across the carpet and my cheek burns. I have to blink numerous times to stop the spinning that is threatening to make me pass out. Kane's fingers tangle in my hair, and he lifts me off the ground, screaming.

"Let me go!" I wail, lashing out and kicking his shin.

He roars in pain and stumbles backward. I charge toward the door, but a shot rings out, and before I can do anything more a burning pain cripples my leg, sending me dropping to the ground again. I scream. I scream so loudly that Kane roars at me to shut up. Blood soaks my leg, and it feels as though a hot poker is being driven in and out of my thigh. I roll around, gasping for air as the pain becomes too much.

"Please," Eric whispers. "Stop."

"Fucking bitch," Kane bellows, driving his foot into my ribs. "I'll fucking kill you for everything you put me through. I was in prison for fucking years because of you."

He storms toward me, but I roll at the last minute. It takes all my strength to move, because I'm in so much pain, but I won't die like this. I won't let him kill me. He spins when I roll, and I drive my fist up into his groin, bringing him to his knees with a pained roar. The gun tumbles from his hand, and when it hits the floor we all dive for it. Eric makes it first, lifting it with trembling hands. His face is as white as a ghost's.

Kane leaps at me, landing on my back and flattening me into the carpet. I scream and try to scurry forward, but he has me pinned. "I'll fucking kill you, you fucking whore!" he roars. I see the glimmer of a knife, and I know I have a split second before Kane drives it into my back and ends me.

"Eric, shoot him!" I scream.

The next moment of my life happens in slow motion. The knife Kane has obviously pulled out is plunged toward me just as Eric pulls the trigger. Kane jerks, and his body rolls off mine, and I hear his bellows of pain. I slump in shock, unable to move, unable to escape it. Eric rushes over, dropping to his knees beside me.

"Indigo, are you okay?" he frantically cries.

Aside from the burning pain in my leg, I am.

"You need to go and get help, Eric. Now."

"I..."

"Eric, get it before he stops screaming and decides to make me pay for you shooting him."

Eric nods frantically and shoves the gun into my hands as I push to my feet. Then he turns and bolts out the door. I have minutes. I stare down at Kane, and anger swells in my chest. He came in here, knowing full well one of us wouldn't come out alive. I know it too, and I decided the moment that bullet hit my leg that it wouldn't be me. I watch as he lifts his head. Blood pours from his neck, and when he smiles that sick, evil smile, his teeth are covered in blood.

"You couldn't do it," he snarls. "You'd never live with yourself."

"See," I snap, pointing the gun at him. "That's where you've always been wrong about me. When it comes to monsters, there is no hesitation."

"You're a fucking weak who—"

His voice is cut off when I pull the trigger. The bullet hits him right between the eyes, and his body slumps to the ground. I stand there a moment in complete shock.

I'm not sure what I expected to feel when I ended Kane's life. I know I have only minutes, so I quickly drop the gun and turn, rushing toward the motel door. I reach it and open it, peering out quickly. The guards are grouped off toward the front of the hotel, and Eric is frantically yelling at them.

I look to my left and see the thick trees. I have to go toward those; it's my only hope. I have to figure out a plan, but I need to be away from here to do it. I can't think about my actions. If I do, I'll panic.

I run out of the motel, and my leg throbs in pain. It's not enough to stop me, though, and adrenalin pumps through my veins as I reach the small wire fence and leap over it, landing with a thump on the other side. I can hear boots crunching and voices yelling out, and I know they're about to discover a dead Kane in my room.

I begin to run through the thick of the trees, shoving and pushing branches and twigs aside to get past as quickly as I can. They're thick, and the ground is wet, but I keep shoving through it. The trees thicken the farther in I get, and it feels like I run for over an hour before they begin to thin out. I squint my eyes through the sweat that's pouring down my forehead and see there's a clearing ahead. Thank God. I shove through the trees farther, and when I finally reach the clearing I launch myself out, not even bothering to look first.

As soon as I am in view, my eyes fall on a large very familiar ship. Oh. Shit. I frantically let my eyes travel to the deck of that ship, where I see a familiar face. Drake. His eyes widen when he sees me, and he yells something. I can't go back with them, even though they're likely the only chance I have at avoiding life in jail. I can't risk being sold after everything I went through. I just can't. Panic swells in my chest, and the reality of the situation hits me like a brick. I killed a man.

Oh God.

I am a murderer.

I turn quickly, and I run.

"Indi, stop," Drake yells.

I charge back toward the trees, and glance back just as I reach them, only to see Hendrix literally leap over the side of the ship. The bastard lands on his feet and charges toward me. Oh, fuck. I pick up my pace, shoving back through the thick trees. I reach a giant tree stump on the ground, and I go to leap over it, only to land face-first in a muddy puddle. I cry out and push myself to my hands and knees, scurrying forward, but moments later, a body flattens me back into that puddle. I squirm and kick, screaming and fighting.

"Indigo, stop!" Hendrix yells into my ear as he pins me down.

"No, no, no, no," I cry.

"Enough," he orders, lifting himself off the ground and taking me with him. Then I'm up and over his shoulder before I get the chance to fight harder.

I pummel my fists into his back, screaming and squirming, as he carries me back out and toward the trees.

"Get the ship out. We move now!" he bellows.

"Let me go, no, please, Hendrix, please."

"Hush," he barks.

He carries me to the ladder and shoves me up. Drake leans down, gripping my shoulders and lifting me effortlessly. He wraps his big arms around me, holding me tight even though I'm screaming and clawing. Hendrix appears moments later, and I clench my eyes shut, refusing to look at him.

"She's bleeding. Get her below deck."

"No, please, no!" I scream.

Drake literally drags me below deck, kicking and screaming, and when we get into Hendrix's room, and they're both in, he lets me go. I charge toward the door, but Hendrix has me in a second, pinning me to him. His big arms curl around my body and he holds me so tightly I can hardly breathe. My head spins, and I feel like I'm about to hyperventilate. I am shaking, and my teeth are clattering with shock.

"Enough. If you don't stop I'll get Jess to sedate you."

"I don't want to be on here. Please don't do this to me. Please, I have to go. Don't sell me. Hendrix, please. I don't want it. I hate you. I fucking hate you, because I love you. I hate you. Let me go. Please. Let me go. I have to run. I killed him. I have to run. Don't sell me."

My babbling is frantic, my mind is spinning, and I feel like I'm about to explode with emotion. My chest is tight with panic and I can't breathe.

"You . . . what did you say?" he rasps into my ear.

"Cap, she's in shock. She's panicking. You need to calm her down."

"Get Jess," Hendrix orders.

Drake leaves the room, and Hendrix wrestles me over to the bed. He drops me down onto it before planting his body over mine.

"Look at me, Indigo."

"Let me go," I wail, shaking my head from side to side. "Let me go, Hendrix please."

"Stop it," he says calmly. "Baby, stop."

"Let me go. Hate you. Love you. Killed him."

My babbling is out of control, and my head is spinning so much I feel sick. I begin to retch, and Hendrix curses. Moments later, I hear more familiar voices.

"She's panicking and rambling. I think she's in shock." I hear Hendrix say.

"Hold her still. I'll inject her with this to calm her."

Jess.

"Jess!" I cry, feeling my hands grasp at nothing.

"I'm here, baby. It's okay, you're okay. Just hold still for me."

I feel someone grip my arm, and then I feel a sting of pain.

A moment later, my world spins, and I'm swallowed back into the darkness.

CHAPTER SIXTEEN

I flicker my eyes open, and all I see for a moment is blurred light. I blink once, twice, and slowly reality dawns on me. I'm on Hendrix's ship again. How the hell did I do such a 360 in a few short days? How did he even know I was on that island? Oh, who am I kidding? Our faces were plastered all over the news. Kane managed to find me in a day. Thinking of Kane has me shuddering and wrapping my arms around myself.

One thing at a time.

I can't stay on this ship. I haven't fought this hard to go backward.

I slowly rise and peer around the room. He's not in here, thank God. I slide my feet off the bed, and my leg aches. I stare down at it and see it's been bandaged. I bet Jess did that. My mind is hazy about what happened after I found Hendrix. I was so panicked it's just a blur to me. I lift my fingers to feel my swelling cheek and sigh. I can't think about Kane right now. I can't. I just . . . can't. I find myself some clothes and pull them on before walking to the door and peering out.

The halls are empty.

I step out and walk toward the deck. I'll take the risk; I'll get in that damned lifeboat and take the risk. I am beyond pretending, and I won't let myself be sold. When I step up on the deck I see Hendrix and Drake standing at the end of the ship, talking quietly together. When they notice me, both men stop talking. I back up. Drake looks at Hendrix, but his eyes are burning into mine.

"Go below deck. Don't let anyone up here."

Drake nods and walks off, giving me a quick gentle smile before disappearing. I turn my gaze back to Hendrix, and he slowly begins walking toward me.

"Don't do this," I whisper. "Just let me go, Hendrix."

"I can't do that, *inocencia*," he says in a careful tone.

"Just let me go. I will find a way off. I won't let you hold me here."

He stops in front of me and reaches out, but I shove at him and duck past him. Rushing to the side of the ship.

"There is no way off. You know that."

I spin around, shaking with emotion. "I hate you! I fucking hate you. Just let me go. Don't make me become someone's sex slave. I don't deserve this."

My entire body begins to tremble, and tears rush down my cheeks. He seems shocked by my crying, and he tilts his head to the side, studying me.

"Inocencia," he begins.

"Fuck you!" I scream, rushing toward the door. He catches me before I can get to it, and he wraps his big arms around my body and squeezes me close.

"Let me go," I hiss. "Just let me go."

"Listen to me," he orders.

"Fuck you, pirate!"

"Indigo . . ."

"No," I scream, shoving him so hard he takes two steps back. "I won't listen to you. All you're going to do is make me feel incomplete. Do you know that you can do that? Make someone feel so utterly worthless? You touched me like I mattered, and yet you look at me like I'm a sale. I won't do it. I don't deserve it. I don't . . ."

He's moving toward me before I can finish, and before I know what's happening he grips my shoulder and jerks me forward, crushing his lips down on mine.

My world stops.

My legs give way.

Hendrix wraps his arms around my waist, holding me up before parting my shocked frozen lips with his tongue. It only takes a moment for me to respond. My entire body is tingling with warmth, my heart is thumping, and my stomach is full of butterflies. I open my mouth to him, and I let him slide his tongue inside. I connect my tongue with his and, finally, I get to taste him. It's been worth the wait. His lips, his tongue, his mouth: it's like heaven. The feeling of his stubble on my cheeks is exactly as I imagined.

He makes a throaty sound and pushes my body up against the side of the ship, and the frenzy takes over both of us. I grip the back of his neck, urging him closer, and he leans down, gripping my pants and shoving them down.

I don't stop kissing him. I can't. I whimper into his mouth, and a warm gush of salty air causes my hair to flick around. He lifts one hand, grabbing the thick locks and tugging my head back. His mouth slides from mine, and I groan in disapproval. He chuckles huskily and continues moving my pants. Then his lips are on mine again, hard, desperate, hungry.

He grips his jeans, jerking them down, and then he lifts my leg over his hip before shoving my panties aside. I hear the crackling of a condom wrapper and then he's pressed against my entrance. Oh, yes. He grips my ass, his fingers bite into my flesh, and then he impales me in one swift movement. I cry out, letting his lips go to throw my head back. His other hand grips the back of my head, keeping it tilted so he can find my neck with his lips. Then he pulls out and drives into me again.

"Oh God," I whimper. "Hendrix."

"So fuckin' wet," he growls against my neck, thrusting again.

The one leg that is still on the ground begins to buckle, and I grip the side of the ship for balance. Hendrix releases my hair, places his hand on the railing, and begins to thrust harder, faster. I scream, my sex clenches, and my body tingles with need. His hand is still on my ass, using it to drive each thrust, making sure my hips are tilted on that perfect angle. I feel my pussy clench and those bolts of pleasure start coming in closer and closer together until I explode.

"Oh, God!" I scream.

"Aw, fuck," Hendrix roars.

Together we come, as if our bodies are in sync. I can feel every jerk of his cock, and I have no doubt he can feel every clench of my pussy. He slowly releases my ass, and my leg slides down. He wraps his arm around my waist, but keeps me pressed against the side of the ship. I drop my head into his chest, and breathe him in.

"I changed my mind," he murmurs into my hair. "I'm not selling you, Indigo."

I lift my head, and meet his gaze. "But why?"

He looks out to the ocean for a moment before turning back to me. "Because you do something to me, right here," he says, thumping his chest, right over his heart. "And one thing I've learned in my life is that when something affects your heart, you don't let it go. There are only so many times in life that something can have that effect on a person."

I feel my entire body swell with . . . is that love?

Am I in love with Hendrix?

"The minute I saw you running I knew I had made a fucking mistake. It burned watching you swim away from me, and it was in that moment that I knew you had gotten deeper than I thought. You're something to me, *inocencia*. I'm not quite sure what that something is yet, but I'm not lettin' you go."

"Why do you call me that?" I whisper.

"Because it's what you are, Indigo," he murmurs, stroking a stray piece of hair from my forehead. "You are innocence."

Innocence.

I'm not innocence anymore.

∽

"Sit," Hendrix says, and I stare around at the room of pirates.

I sit down, and he stands beside me, gripping the back of my chair. "We may have a problem on our hands, and we may not. I don't know how it'll go yet, but I do know that we need to be alert. Indigo did something back on that island that could come back to bite her, and we're going to be here to protect her."

I shudder and wrap my arms around myself. Jess lifts her chair and scoots it over beside me, taking my hand. I'm grateful to her right now.

"Indi, we need you to give us a rundown of what happened and who heard it," Hendrix says, staring down at me.

I swallow and turn my eyes away. I haven't spoken about Kane yet. I haven't said the words, not even to Hendrix.

I am a murderer.

I close my eyes and speak as loudly as I can. "He found me because he saw my face all over the news. He saw Eric, used him to get to my motel room. There was a fight. Eric got the gun and shot him in the neck. I told Eric to go get help, and then . . ."

I shiver, and Hendrix grips my shoulder, squeezing gently.

"Keep goin' baby."

"I shot him. I knew I was going to, I knew I had to. I sent Eric away so he wouldn't witness it. I told him to go and get help, and then I shot him and ran. I saw the officers huddled when I went out of the motel, but they didn't see me. I ran, and that's when I found you."

"Did you leave the gun?" Hendrix asks.

"Y . . . y . . . yes."

"Chances are they will put it down to self-defense if it came down to it, but you running didn't help. I have outside sources. I will see what I can find out about the case."

"I'm assuming we now have to deal with Chopper, too?" Drake asks.

Chopper.

I shudder.

The idea of that man just makes me feel ill, and I haven't even seen him.

Hendrix turns and stares at me, and there's something in his face . . . something . . . Is that pity? Why is he looking at me like that?

"*Inocencia*, we have to talk about that. There's something you need to know."

I shake my head, confused. "I thought . . . you weren't selling me?"

My entire body coils tightly, and I struggle to breathe. Did he change his mind? Was he only lying to me?

"Hey," he says, dropping down in front of me. "I'm not selling you, but there is something that concerns you in regard to Chopper."

"What has Chopper got to do with me?"

He sighs deeply, lifting a hand to rub his forehead. Then he gets to his feet and glances at Drake.

"Cap, what's going on?"

Hendrix stares at nothing for a moment then turns to me again. "You remember when we were talking before you ran away on the island?"

"Yes."

"And do you remember telling me your father's name?"

Where is he going with this? Oh God, did Chopper kill my father? I feel my skin prickle as I meet Hendrix's eyes. "I . . . yes."

"Indigo," he begins. Oh God, he's using my full name. This is bad, very bad. "Chopper . . . is your father."

The entire room breaks out in confused chatter and gasps.

Me, I can't do anything but gape.

Did he just say Chopper is my father?

He's wrong. My father isn't a filthy pirate. He's a kind, beautiful man who left me. Hendrix has it wrong. He can't be right. He has the wrong name, or maybe it's just a coincidence. It can't be true. I stare down at my hands, and they're shaking. Why are they shaking? I don't believe him. He's wrong. He's got this all wrong.

"You're wrong," I whisper. "My father is gone. He's not a pirate."

"Chopper's real name is Charles Waters, Indigo."

"It's a coincidence then," I bark suddenly, getting to my feet.

"I might say the same, except when I think about it . . . he's just like you. Indi, he looks like you."

My hands shake and my jaw clenches. How dare he? How dare he stand here in a room full of people and tell such rotten lies? If he's right, he's saying the father I adored is a raping pig who takes women and sells them. I can't believe that to be right. I won't believe it.

"You're lying!" I scream. "Is this your way of getting back at me for running? Is this your punishment?"

"Indigo," he says almost gently. "I'm telling you because you deserve to know."

"You're wrong!" I roar. "My daddy is a good man. I know him."

"Indi . . ."

"No," I hiss, putting my hand up. "You don't get to do this in a room full of people. If you wanted to make me pay, Hendrix, you've done a great job at it."

"Jesus, Indi, do you honestly think I would be such an ass? I'm not telling you a fucking lie."

"Then why are you telling me?" I whimper, crumbling. Jess is by my side, rubbing my back. I didn't even notice until now.

"Because you have the right to know."

"To know what? That every image of my father has just been shattered?"

"Indi . . ."

"Let me take her," Jess says softly. "I'll talk to her."

Hendrix's eyes are pleading with me, but I don't understand. I don't. He nods, and Jess wraps an arm around my shoulder and turns me around, leading me out into the hall. She walks me slowly to her room and opens the door, encouraging me in. We sit on her bed, and she turns to me.

"I don't think he's lying, honey. Hendrix doesn't say things unless he knows."

"It can't be true, Jess," I whisper, feeling my lip quiver.

"It might not be how you think it is. Maybe your dad isn't so bad."

"He was going to sell me to him as a sex slave," I cry, shaking. "It doesn't get much worse."

"Maybe he doesn't sell them, or . . ."

"Jess, just stop. I love you for caring, but you can't take away the reality of this situation."

"I know, honey . . ."

"I just don't want to see it, even if he is right. My dad was everything to me, and even after he left me I still loved him so much.

I don't want that image shattered. I don't want to see him the way Hendrix has described him. I can't . . ."

"Until you do see him, you're not going to know what is real and what isn't."

"I know," I whisper. "I just feel numb right now. This is all too much to take in. My life has never been easy, but I dealt with it, and I made the most of it . . . then I came here, and everything I believed in has been stomped on. I killed someone, Jess . . ."

She lifts her gaze to mine, and nods. "I know, honey."

"I'm a murderer," I whisper.

"No, you're a woman protecting herself."

A tear slides down my cheek, and I struggle to keep my composure. "I love him, Jess."

"I know you do, baby."

"I don't know what to do . . ."

"I know what you have to do," she murmurs. "You have to keep on surviving, and take each day as it comes."

If only it were that easy.

CHAPTER SEVENTEEN

A warm hard body slides into the bed beside me and I shudder before pressing myself into it. I'm hurt by what Hendrix told me earlier, but my need for him is so strong. I feel him run his big hand up my side and then he grips the back of my head, pulling my lips down on his.

I wonder if kissing him will ever get old? The feeling that's flooding my body right now seems like it couldn't possibly fade. It gets stronger each time he lays his hands on me.

His lips are warm, and he tastes like rum. The burn of the alcohol as I open my mouth and let our tongues dance is quite enjoyable. I lift my hands, wrapping them in his hair and tugging him closer. He makes a growling sound, and his hand slides back down my body until he grips my backside, pulling me to him. I throw one leg over his hips, and our bodies touch. His cock presses against my pussy, and the friction of his jeans does wonderful things to me.

I never thought it possible to want someone so much, until him. I can't get enough of what he has to offer. He gives it, and I can't stop taking. He pulls his lips from mine, and I can feel his warm breath tickling my cheek as he moves down to my ear. "I've fucked you, *inocencia*, and I've made your body come alive, but I haven't given you the one thing I know you need."

What do I need?

"And that is?" I pant.

"I haven't made love to you."

Oh.

Sweet.

Jesus.

I've seen Hendrix's tough side, I've seen him kill in cold blood, I've seen the monster that lies within, but the other side to him almost easily outweighs it. He has this gentle side, a side that is so sweet, and yet he makes it so damned masculine.

"Y . . . y . . . you . . . want to make love to me?"

"I want nothing more," he murmurs, and then moves his lips down my neck.

No one has ever made love to me.

They say it's different, that when someone makes love to you it truly defines sex and what it's about. I've been fucked by Hendrix, and it was mind-blowing—I really couldn't imagine it getting any better. Yet something inside me is telling me that I'm about to find out I'm very wrong about that. When Hendrix runs his fingers up the side of my body, so slowly, so gently, I know for a fact that I'm wrong. I know without a doubt in my heart . . .

That this will change something inside me.

Hendrix removes my clothes so slowly, so gently, that I can barely feel his hands on me. When I'm naked, he strips out of his clothes and then flicks the dim lamp on beside the bed. My heart begins to hammer. When he's looking down at me like that, with those eyes, and that damned stunning face, it's hard to think of anything else. He leans down, and presses a tiny kiss to my nose. I smile and for the first time since I've been here, he smiles too. It's not a grin, or a smirk; it's a genuine, heart-wrenchingly beautiful smile.

It just confirms what I'm sure I already figured out.

Hendrix is everything I need.

I reach up and cup his face before murmuring, "I need to kiss you again. You starved me for too long."

His smile turns lopsided and I nearly sigh with want. "Kiss away, sweetheart."

He lowers his mouth, and I capture his lips with mine, kissing him softly. Our lips move in the most sensual way, and every now and then he nips at my bottom lip. I let him push me back into the mattress and press his body over mine. He gently pulls away from my lips and moves his mouth down, sliding his body down mine until he finds my breasts. He captures his nipple in my mouth, and he sucks, drawing it in and out of his mouth and flicking it with his tongue.

"More," I whimper, arching up, pushing my nipples farther into his mouth.

His fingers run across the smooth skin on my hip as he devours my nipples, and I bite my lip to stop the desperate moan escaping. His fingers trace little circles on my leg before slowly moving up my thigh, gently caressing, teasing me. He releases my nipple and lifts his brown eyes to meet mine. His look is questioning, as if asking me if I want more. I make a strangled moaning sound and he grins, slowly lowering his head and trailing kisses down my belly. My skin breaks out in tiny little shivers and my legs become tense. Oh, the anticipation.

He has my sex aching, desperate for him, and then he moves down past it. The need for him to put his mouth on me is overwhelming. "Please Hendrix," I mewl.

"Soon, baby."

He slides down to my toes, where he pops one into his mouth. The sudden throaty moan that escapes my lips has him chuckling. He kisses the ball of my foot, and then slowly drags his lips up my legs, kissing, stroking, kneading my skin with his palms. I close my eyes and let my head drop into the pillow. This . . . it's different. My heart is aching, my body is aware of his every movement, and the need to devour him is sending me over the edge.

He moves his lips up the inside of my thigh and inhales. "Fuckin' perfect."

"Please," I beg, arching my hips off the bed.

"Hush," he murmurs, sliding his tongue out, and just touching the skin on the inside of my thigh.

Everything clenches, and my pussy begins to throb.

He moves his mouth closer, and I can feel his hot breath against my skin. Then, slowly, he dips his tongue into my exposed flesh and gently slides it up and around my clit. I begin to pant and my fingers grip the sheet, holding it so tightly they ache. I thrash my head from side to side, needing more. Hendrix presses harder, his tongue putting just enough pressure on to cause my clit to send a bolt of pleasure up my spine. I rasp his name and spread my legs wider, thrusting my hips up.

"*Inocencia* likes having her sweet pussy licked," he breathes into my skin.

"Please," I beg again. "Hendrix, please . . ."

"All in good time, baby."

He closes his mouth over my clit and I jerk wildly, mewling and arching. He sucks it into his mouth, still flicking it with his tongue. Heat fills my body and my pussy begins to tighten and swell. Oh. Yes. When he gently slides his finger inside my no doubt damp entrance, I come. For a moment, I am incoherent as I whimper his name and he continues to draw every last shudder from my body. Then he's moving up, sliding his hard flesh over mine until he reaches my lips again.

He dips his head and he slides his tongue into my mouth. I close my lips over it and I suck, tasting myself, tasting what he does to me. He growls, and his hands slide up and cup my head, lifting it slightly so he can deepen the kiss. He might not be able to tell me what I mean to him, but he's showing me. Every kiss. Every touch. Every stroke of his hand against my skin. He's showing me that he cares. He's giving me what he can't tell me.

"Make love to me," I whisper, pulling back and cupping his cheek.

He closes his eyes, as if the very thought brings some sort of pain to his heart. He releases my head and slides his hands down my body, gripping my thigh and bringing it up and over his hip. Then he's pressing against me, ever so gently, just probing my entrance, promising me pleasure but not going over the edge.

"I'm unprotected, Indigo," he murmurs.

"I don't care, I want you . . . all of you."

He makes a throaty sound, and then he gently slides inside. My body tightens around him as an overwhelming sensation travels through my body. It's that of something that's real. Something pure. Something that's just ours.

Hendrix drops his lips to mine again and he kisses me deeply as he begins to gently thrust. His body moves in and out of mine, and I can feel every inch of him on my skin. His muscles tense and pull when he does, and a fine layer of sweat breaks out on his skin.

He runs his hands up my arms, bringing them above my head. I drop my head back, mouth open, little whimpers escaping. I've never felt anything like this in my life. It's a feeling that consumes not only my body but my heart. It's the perfect balance, the perfect match. It's a connection.

"So beautiful," Hendrix murmurs into my ear as he slides his lips down my neck.

I cry out when his hands slide down and cup my cheeks. He's holding onto me, his muscles are straining, his jaw is tight, and his eyes are locked on mine. It's a moment that's so beautiful, so utterly perfect. He slides his thumb across the skin on my cheek, swiping a piece of damp hair off my forehead. Our eyes remain locked and we share something there in that moment, something uncontaminated by past pains and regrets. I close my eyes as my body swells with warmth and I climb closer to the edge.

"Eyes, Indigo," he rasps. "Always on me."

I open them and meet his once more, and what I see in them has my womb clenching with need. It's gentle compassion, a loving glance that no heated look could ever compare to. He leans down, sliding his tongue over my bottom lip as he continues to rock his hips into me. I feel my orgasm nearing closer to the edge, and I know it's going to be unlike anything I've ever felt. There's added warmth in my body that was never there before.

"H . . . Hendrix," I say gasping. "N . . . now."

He tilts his hips and sends me over the edge. Stars explode in my vision as wave after wave of pleasure travels through my body. I can't even scream—all I can do is open my mouth and whimper his name over and over again. He is whispering in my ear, and his body is so tense I can feel every muscle against my skin, but he doesn't pick up the pace and slam into me, he slowly rocks himself until he's letting off an almost pained yell.

He drops his head into my shoulder, and together we lie there, panting, both of our bodies on overload from a pleasure I imagine we have both never felt before. I lift my hand, tangling it in his thick, damp hair. His body is hard, and heavy, but the feeling of him lying over me, his chest rising and falling, is wonderful. I slide my hands down his cheeks and make little circles there with my thumbs.

He lifts his head and stares down at me, stroking the hair from my forehead. "Here I was thinking I could teach you something, and yet it was the complete opposite. You taught me something tonight, *inocencia*."

"What's that?" I whisper.

"You taught me how to open my heart."

I swallow and reach up, stroking his face.

"You know what, pirate?" I murmur, meeting his eyes. "You taught me that too."

~

"I've been looking for you."

I hear Senny's voice and turn to see her standing in the hall with her arms crossed. I haven't had a lot of trouble from Senny since Hendrix threatened her, but I didn't imagine it would last long. She stalks toward me, her nose scrunched up, her eyes full of hate. What did I ever do to deserve such hatred from her? When she stops in front of me, she looks me up and down as if I'm no more than a piece of trash.

"Can I help you, Sienna?" I mutter.

"I want a word."

"I don't believe we have anything to talk about."

"We have plenty to talk about."

I cross my arms and lean against the wall. "And what would that be?"

"I know he's chosen you and I don't honestly care. I've fucked him enough times to know what he's offering, and to be honest, I can do better."

I snort. She glares.

"What I am here to do is tell you that you have no idea what you're getting yourself into with Hendrix."

"I think I can figure those things out on my own, thanks."

She grins, and it's mean. "See, here's the thing, princess. You have no idea what his life is like. Has he even told you how he ended up here, or why he owes your dear daddy money?"

I flinch at her using the word *daddy*.

I haven't processed that yet.

"I don't really care. If you think I'm so naive that I don't know Hendrix has done bad things, along with my father, then you really don't know me. Now, I know exactly what you're doing: you're trying to make me feel insecure because you lost, but honey, nothing you can say will change my mind about him."

Her grin widens, and that almost frightens me.

"He's got a kid, you know?"

And there it goes, that blow to the chest that makes you want to fall onto the ground and never get back up.

A kid.

A kid.

My head spins, but I struggle to keep my face straight and unaffected.

"Are you done?" I say, glaring at her.

Her grin drops. The stupid bitch is confused because I'm not on the ground sobbing and crying.

"There's more . . ."

"More that I really don't want to hear about. Now, if you're finished, I would like to go," I growl, turning and walking off.

"You'll regret being with him," she cries. "You will! Just ask what happened to his ex-wife."

Another blow, a big one.

Bigger than the kid.

I gasp, but keep walking. When I get around the corner, my legs tremble and I grip the wall for support. A child. A wife. Why didn't he tell me any of this? How did I not know he was married and had a child? A child! I close my eyes, trying to gather my calm. Don't judge until you know the story, don't judge until you know the story . . . I repeat this over and over, all while trying to catch my breath and stop the ache in my heart.

"Indi?"

I open my eyes to see Hendrix watching me. He looks concerned; his eyebrows are furrowed.

"You okay?"

"Is it true?" I whisper. "Do you have a kid?"

His jaw tenses and he sighs loudly, looking down at the floor.

"Is it?" I say, as calmly as I can.

"It's a long story. Come on."

He grips my arm and tugs me, and I let him. He leads me up onto the deck and barks at everyone to fuck off before he takes us over to an old bench that's bolted to the ground. We sit down, and he turns to face me.

"I don't even know where to start. I haven't told this story for so many years. I know exactly who told you, and believe me when I say I'm not happy about it. She will get her ass kicked for it later, but you know now, so I guess I need to give you some answers. Firstly, he's not my kid, not biologically."

I'm just confused now. He sees it in my face, and continues.

"When I was fifteen years old, I was in a bad place. Most fifteen-year-old boys are out with their friends, enjoying life. I was battling to survive. My parents were dead, and I was on the street with no family. One night, I met a girl. She was twenty-one and basically a prostitute. She took me in one night after seeing me on the street. She must have felt sorry for me, because she let me stay and we got together. She had a five-year-old son. His dad was dead and he had nothing. I fell into a relationship, and eventually, over the years, the boy began to call me Dad. I was with them until I was twenty-five, so a solid ten years.

"I married Lizzie when I was twenty years old. I was just a kid still, but she was all I had. Her and Dimitri. We managed together, but Lizzie was a heavy drug addict, and she got herself tangled into some serious shit. By this stage, I had started sailing and creating myself a crew of pirates to begin dealing with her problems out at sea. It's easier out here. Less law. The reason I got into it was an old friend of mine had association with some pirates, and he got me involved, promising it would be the best option for Lizzie and Dimitri. He was right; it was easier. So, basically, I got involved in the pirate world to save a woman who really didn't care about me or her son. I was working hard to pay off her drug debts, trying to make a better life for them.

"Things got so bad that eventually I realized I couldn't help her anymore, and I left. I became a full-time pirate. Dimitri thought I was his father. He didn't know any better, and I loved him. I was selfish, because I left him with no explanation. I kept tabs on him at all times, making sure he was okay, making sure he was protected, but one day when he was fifteen my sources came back to me and told me he was in the hospital. He'd been so badly beaten and . . . raped . . . that he was in a coma. I went mad. The woman had tangled herself up so much that her own son had copped it. So I paid a well-known pirate to put a hit on her."

"My father," I whisper.

"Yeah, he had his men take her out. It went wrong, and they ended up having to take out more than just her. That's why he's chasing me for payment; he didn't get enough for the job they had to do. I wasn't giving it to him. We had a deal. After she was gone, I went into the hospital to see Dimitri. He was awake, broken, and completely damaged. He hated me. He thought I was the reason his mother had nothing and got herself into such a bad place that she got killed. He swore then and there that he would kill me for it one day. I left, and since then I haven't seen him again."

Oh, God.

"I'm so sorry," I whisper. "I know how much it must hurt."

"He might not have been my son, but I loved him like he was. I know what I did to him. I know the damage I put into him. I also know the damage that was done the day he got beaten and raped. His soul is darkness, and I'm sure by now it's consumed him. I tried to keep tabs on him, but he disappeared, and I lost track of him."

"It's such an awful thing to happen to someone," I say, gripping his hand.

"Yeah, and the fucked-up thing is that I could have taken him with me on the ship, but I thought he was better off with his momma."

"Sometimes we make mistakes, Hendrix. It's human nature. So long as we learn from those mistakes then we should be forgiven for them."

He shakes his head and grips my face, pulling me close. "How'd you get so fuckin' smart?"

I smile. "I didn't. It's just reality."

"Hmmmm," he murmurs, pressing his lips to mine for a moment. "Well, you make reality sound awesome."

I giggle, and he pulls me into his arms.

So many stories, so many endings.

I wonder what my ending will be?

CHAPTER EIGHTEEN

"Have another one, lassie." GG grins, pouring me another rum. I giggle and shoot it back. The liquid burns my throat. Warmth floods my veins, and my giggling intensifies.

"You're going to get into trouble soon." I laugh. "Hendrix is watching you."

He smirks and wraps an arm around me. "I love his jealous side."

I laugh loudly. "Me too."

"Dance with me, scallywag."

I snort and roll my eyes, "That's my joke!"

"Well, you're one of us now, so I can use it against you."

"Fair enough." I grin, taking his hand and leading him out to the middle of the room. We begin to dance, wiggling our hips to the music on the radio.

I catch a glimpse of Hendrix every now and then, and the look in his eyes is purely sexual. He's grinning at me, and every now and then he shakes his head as I do a saucy dance move. I turn slowly and begin wiggling toward him. He's sitting in a chair at the back of the room, and when he sees me approaching he lifts his hands and puts them up behind his head. A lazy smirk appears on his lips as I shimmy closer. He lifts his hand, and crooks his finger, encouraging me toward him. I shake my head and keep grinning as I move.

His smile gets bigger and he pats his leg. I shake my head again.

And so the challenge starts.

He crooks his finger again, and I continue to dance in circles, shimmying around him and refusing to do as he asks. With a smirk, he gets to his feet and begins stalking toward me, looking like sex on legs. When he reaches me, I spin away just as he stretches his hand out. Chuckling, he lashes out and catches me, spinning me into him and placing his hands on my hips. Then he begins to grind our bodies together in time with the music.

Oh, yes.

His hips move from side to side, his hands slide down to my backside, and he grips it, making my ass move with his. He's grinning down at me, those big brown eyes connecting with mine. I bite my lip and slide my hands around his waist, finding his shirt and sliding my hands up underneath it to feel the hot hard skin there.

"Get a room," someone yells.

I laugh and reach up, pressing my lips to his. He dips his head, deepening the kiss and sliding his tongue into my mouth. Mmmmm. I will never get tired of kissing him.

"Cap?"

We hear Drake's voice and pull apart. I turn and smile at him, and he gives me a small grin in return.

"What is it, buddy?" Hendrix says, not taking his hands from my ass.

"Meeting is starting in five."

Hendrix nods, and turns to look back down at me. He organized tonight so he could go over some things with the guys, but we girls crashed his party. Well, me and Jess. Though Jess is in the corner with Lenny chatting about something that has her giggling loudly every few minutes.

"Meeting," Hendrix bellows.

The guys stop what they are doing, and all stand, walking over and taking a seat around the large table. I go to walk out, but Hendrix tightens his grip on me. "You're on my lap, revenge for that dance tease you just did."

How is that revenge?

I like his lap.

He leads me over and takes a seat at the head of the table, before pulling me down onto his lap. GG slides me another rum, and I give him an enthusiastic grin. Hendrix reaches out and wraps his fingers around the glass and slides it back, lifting it and bringing it to his lips.

"Hey!" I pout. "That's mine."

"Mine now, baby."

I purposely shift on his lap, making sure my bottom grinds against his cock. He tenses up and puts a hand on my leg, squeezing it.

"Behave," he murmurs into my ear before starting.

"You boys know the drill. It's our usual weekly meeting. I want ideas on stock, where we're at with navigation, any other shit that has gone down. GG, go . . ."

GG begins speaking, and for a moment I listen. That is, until Hendrix slides his hand up my leg until he reaches the hem of my dress. I stiffen. He wouldn't do that here? Would he?

He would. He slides his fingers up the inside of my thigh. When I go to shift, he wraps his hand around my middle and holds me tightly against him. His fingers skim my panties, and then he gently pushes my legs open a little, all the while nodding and answering GG as though he doesn't have his fingers against my pussy.

"So that's it for stock," GG says.

"Lenny?" Hendrix asks, slipping his finger into my panties and finding my slick sex.

Oh. Shit.

Lenny begins talking, and Hendrix continues to act like nothing is happening. Me, I am struggling to stop myself writhing against him and crying out his name. He slides his finger up and down my slit, gathering moisture, and then makes little circles on my clit. I tense up, chewing on my tongue to stop any sounds coming out. I pretend to focus on the glass in front of me, but it soon becomes blurred as my vision swims. Pleasure swells in my womb, and I continue my struggle to keep quiet.

"What about you, Indi?" GG asks. "Have you got everything you need?"

He's talking to me? Oh no.

"Yeah Indi," Hendrix purrs into my ear. "Better give us a list or you'll miss out."

I hate him right now, and I can't even tell him that because I'm afraid if I open my mouth the only thing that will come out is a pathetic cry.

"Well?" GG asks.

"I . . . I . . ."

"You got enough of all that girly bullshit?"

Hendrix places his thumb on my clit and uses his forefinger to thrust into my pussy.

"Girly shit?" Hendrix encourages.

"I . . . um . . . I think I'm okay," I whisper, still focusing on the glass.

"No shampoo or hair brushes . . ."

"Um . . ."

God, he's thrusting deeply, slowly, oh God, it feels so good.

"Y . . . y . . . yes," I say, though I'm sure it's more because of the pleasure than an answer to his question.

"How about you just order everything for the girls that they need," Lenny adds.

"Right," GG says, writing a list of things down.

Hendrix keeps thrusting and rubbing until I'm trying desperately to stop the orgasm that's hanging on the edge. It's there, just waiting to be released, needing to be let go, but I refuse to have it here in front of a group of pirates. As if Hendrix realizes this is what I'm doing, he begins to rub harder and harder. Dammit, I can't hold it back. I'm trying but I can't . . . it feels so good. So fucking good. With one last thrust of his finger, I'm coming, hard. I cough loudly, and cover my mouth as if pretending to contain it. I drop my head and force another cough as my body shudders.

"You okay, lass? Drink too much rum?" someone asks.

I can't answer. If I lift my eyes they will see the pleasure in them. I just nod my head as the last shudders leave my body. Hendrix rubs one last time before sliding his fingers out and pulling my skirt down. Then, as if no one else is in the room, he lifts his fingers above the table and puts one in his mouth. My cheeks flame with heat as I hear the soft suckling sound at my ear. The man has no shame, none at all.

"I should . . . go," I whisper.

"I'll be in soon," Hendrix growls into my ear.

I slide off his lap, and with shaky legs I leave the dining room. Damn him.

I'll get him back for that.

CHAPTER NINETEEN

I know Hendrix is a pirate, but I've never seen him in full pirate action. I've seen him kill a man, and I've seen the dominant side of him, but that's as far as it goes. I have no doubt that he's as utterly terrifying in battle as I would imagine, and I often wonder how many people he's killed out here. He's been out here for so long, delving into illegal things, that there has to be a list. Part of me doesn't want to know because reality can sometimes make us question ourselves, but the other part is desperate for answers.

I get my answer.

We're sleeping. It's late, and Hendrix is pressed against me. I've just dozed off when I hear the ear-shattering boom. As if he's been trained, Hendrix leaps out of the bed. He doesn't stop and think, or take the time to wake: he just gets up and yanks on the closest clothes. I'm still blinking sleep from my eyes when he picks up his gun and loads it. Another boom fills the air, and his eyes dart to the door. This isn't good. Something tells me it won't end well, whatever it is.

"Go into Jess's room. She knows what to do. Take this. Kill anyone you don't know," he says quickly, shoving a gun at me and pulling me out of bed.

He yanks a shirt over my head and hauls my panties up my legs, and I'm still dazed. Shots begin to ring out, and voices begin screaming and yelling down the hall. Sleep leaves quickly then, and panic takes its place. Hendrix races us to the door and flings it open, gun drawn. Drake is just passing us as we step out. "Rogue pirates, Cap. Ten of them, loads of weapons."

"Indi, go to Jess. Do as I asked."

"But . . ."

"Don't argue with me," he hisses. "Just do as you're told."

I nod, swallowing, and rush down the hall to Jess's room. I bang on the door and she opens it quickly, pulling me in. Her face is panicked, and I realize Senny is in here, too. She locks the door and lifts the gun off the table beside her. Seeing the look on her face has my heart seizing and my chest constricting.

"I don't know what's happening," I whisper.

"It's pirates, you idiot," Senny snaps.

"Shut the fuck up, Sienna," Jess barks.

We both stare at her, wide-eyed. I've never heard Jess speak like that, but she's obviously scared, and this is her way of dealing with it. Her eyes don't move from the door, and I find myself shifting over to her, terrified. What if something happens to the guys? What if Hendrix dies? What if they blow up the ship? The thoughts don't do much for my calm, and I end up pushing myself into a state of pure panic.

"It's okay, Indi," Jess says, though she doesn't move from her position at the door.

"I'm frightened."

"I know. It'll be over soon."

I hear the sounds of yelling and gunshots, and even a few screams. I press my hands to my ears and begin to sing loudly. I can't listen—I can't hear it. Jess begins to tap her foot; her face is full of panic and her hands are shaking. Another massive explosion goes off and rocks the ship, causing me to stumble onto the floor along with Senny. Was that our ship that got hit? It settles back into normal floating, and I wait for the smell of a fire, or the gush of water, but it never comes.

The fighting quiets down, and when we can no longer hear it Senny gets to her feet and walks out.

"Seinna!" Jess cries.

"I'm not sitting in here. It's finished."

"Sienna!" I yell. "He said stay in here."

Senny spins just outside of the door and glares at me. "You know nothing, so shut the fuck up. I don't even . . ."

A shot rings out, making a loud crack in the silence, and suddenly Senny stops talking. Her mouth opens and her eyes widen, and then slowly she begins to fall to the floor. Jess screams and the gun topples from her hands. Blood pools around Senny's back as soon as she hits the floor, and her eyes are open, fixed on the ceiling. I know she's dead. I hear the sound of footsteps. Someone is below deck. I dive toward the gun, clutch it in my hands, and then rush over and press my hand over Jess's mouth. The footsteps near and I raise the gun, hands trembling, and wait. I see Senny's body move, and I realize someone has kicked her. Probably checking if she's still alive.

I want to vomit.

I'm so terrified. Nothing in my life has ever frightened me so much. I'm stiff, unable to move, or breathe, or focus. My eyes are on the door, and my hands are firmly clasped around the gun. I see a body first, and I know right away it's not one of Hendrix's men. I don't even think: I just pull the trigger. The man lands with a thump on the ground, rolling and roaring in pain as he grips his stomach.

"Run, Jess!"

Jess scurries past him and drops to her knees by Senny's side.

"Senny? Wake up."

"She's gone," I cry. "Go get help."

With a hiccup, Jess gets to her feet and runs out. The pirate on the ground groans and rolls, getting to his hands and knees. Blood drips from his belly as he begins stalking toward me. I know I should be pulling that trigger right now, but my hands are shaking, and I can't seem to make myself do it. I'm frozen with fear, and only when he lifts his hand to reach for his pants do I know that it's him or me.

I begin to pull the trigger when another gunshot rings out, and suddenly the pirate slumps to the ground. My knees buckle and I fall in a heap, shaking so violently my teeth chatter together. I hear voices, and somewhere in my fear I find myself screaming Hendrix's name. Is he alive? Is he dead? Oh God, what if he's dead? I couldn't live if he died. I don't want to.

"Shhh, Indi, I'm here."

Oh, thank God.

I feel his hard arms go around me and lift me from my spot on the floor. I hear orders being thrown around, and the sound of Jess crying as he carries me past. He places me on his bed in his room, and then moments later Jess is placed beside me. I reach out for her, and she clutches me desperately.

"They're in shock. Just let them be for a minute, Cap," I hear Drake say.

"Feel so fuckin' helpless."

"They got a scare. They saw their friend die. Just let them process that."

Hendrix reaches down and strokes his fingers across my forehead.

"Go and get me Jess's sedatives."

The words are a foggy blur.

Nothing is making a great deal of sense in my head.

I hear shuffling a moment later, and then I feel a sting in my arm.

"Sorry, baby." It's the last thing I hear before I go blank.

The last thing I feel is Jess's hand, trembling in mine.

∼

"May the ocean take her soul and keep her safe for eternity," Drake says.

We watch with blank expressions as they slide Senny's body over the edge of the ship and into the water. Jess is still beside me, her breathing heavy and deep. I know that she and Senny weren't close, but I think for a long time they had only each other on this ship. I reach out and take her hand, and she squeezes it tight while we all lower our heads for a minute, giving Senny the respect she needs right now.

I am trying to ignore the scrubbing sounds behind me, and the smell of bleach that burns my nose as a few of the younger pirates scrub the blood off the deck. I am trying not to focus on it, trying not to think about the reality of the situation that is surrounding me. It's not the fantasy world that people assume it is; it's real, and it's scary. There are things that happen out here that most people wouldn't experience in their lives, and yet these men live it on a daily basis.

This is their world, and now . . . now it's mine.

I'm not sure if this frightens me, or gives me a chance to really discover who I am with a man I adore. He's not what I would have picked for myself but he has changed everything I ever believed I needed. This world is scary, but more than that, it's real. These men believe in everything they are, and they work hard for the things they want. They're criminals, without a doubt, but the passion they hold for each other beats that in some of the families I've seen.

That battle was proof of that. It was also proof of how deadly they truly are. The raid was unsuccessful for the pirates on the other ship, who all ended up as lifeless souls on the bottom of the ocean. By the time I came around, Hendrix had it all sorted out, with no traces left behind except the blood on the deck. Hendrix is that kind of powerful.

"You okay?"

Hendrix comes up behind me and wraps his arms around my waist.

"Yeah, I'm okay."

"It's hard, I know, but I promise you I'll fight every day of my life to make sure nothing happens to you, *inocencia*," he whispers into my ear.

"I know you will."

"Come on, let's get inside. There's some rain coming in."

"Do they . . ." I point to the guys scrubbing the floors. ". . . need help?"

"No, they've got it."

I nod as he turns to Jess. He narrows his eyes and watches as she stares beyond the side of the ship, sobbing, her tiny frame shaking. Letting me go, he walks over and wraps his arms around her, pulling her into him. In that moment I love him that much more. I feel my eyes burn as I watch Jess crumple into him.

"It's going to be okay, Jess. You've got us. We're always going to protect you."

My heart aches for her; it aches so bad. Hendrix lets her go and nods to Drake, who walks over and wraps an arm around her. I watch him lead her away, and I realize these guys are so much more than pirates. They're brothers. They're family. They believe in each other. Pride swells in my chest as I walk over and tuck myself against Hendrix.

"Let's go below deck. I need you . . ."

He wraps his fingers around my arms and leans down, sliding his lips across mine.

"You've got me, always."

That sounds just fine to me.

CHAPTER TWENTY

"Oh, fuck, harder, baby," Hendrix rasps, tangling his hands into my hair.

I slide my mouth up and down his cock, licking, teasing, tormenting him until he's panting and begging me for more. I like hearing him beg. It makes my pussy clench with need. I wrap my hand around the base of his cock and begin gently squeezing. He hisses and jerks his hips, thrusting his cock up into my mouth farther until it's hitting the back of my throat. His feral hiss fills the room, and I find my hand sliding down to cup his balls. My mind goes back to moments when I heard stories about men enjoying having their ass played with. Would a man like Hendrix like something like that?

I test the waters by sliding my finger lower. He tenses for a minute, and his breathing becomes ragged. I run my finger up and down, while sucking, and using my other hand to stroke his cock. I feel him swelling, getting harder and harder in my mouth, and I know he's close. I slip my finger down, gently sliding it in. He growls loudly, and grips my hair. "Fuck, Indi, what are you . . ."

I press into the hard little lump my finger grazes and he's cut off mid-sentence. His words turn into growls and his cock explodes, spurting hard into my mouth. His growling is primal and damned sexy. His hips jerk, and his fingers tighten in my hair as he continues to come, spurting into my throat. My entire body tingles with want as he slowly comes down from his release. He slumps back into the sofa and I gently remove my finger and mouth before sliding up his body and pressing little kisses to his abdomen.

"What the hell was that?" he rasps.

"Just a little trick. Did it work?"

"Are you kidding, baby? Of course it worked."

I giggle, and slide my tongue out and over the hard muscle on his belly.

"Quit doin' that sweetheart, or I'll have to fuck you."

"You can't," I murmur.

"Why not?"

"It's shark week."

He is quiet for a moment, and then he bursts out laughing, his entire body shaking.

"I've heard a lot of things in my time, but fuck, that was gold."

I smile against his belly and look up at him. "You know me, queen of the one-liners."

"Cap?"

Someone bangs on the door and, with an angry sigh, Hendrix jerks up his jeans and gently lifts me off him before standing. "What?"

"There's a ship in the distance."

My skin instantly prickles.

"You identified it?" he says, pulling on a shirt and lifting his gun.

"No."

"On my way."

He turns to me. "Stay here."

"But . . ."

"Indi, stay here."

He kisses my head quickly before turning and rushing out. I stand for a moment, completely terrified. It's been five days since that attack; surely we can't have another one . . .

I rub my arms with my hands and turn, walking toward the bathroom. I clean up, brush my teeth, and put my hair up before making my way back to the sofa and just sitting, waiting, feeling like I'm about to throw up all over the floor.

It feels like I wait for hours, until finally I hear yelling. I get to my feet, feeling my heart pound. The yelling increases, and I recognize a few words. It sounds threatening. Unable to stop myself, I slowly walk out of the room. I should be with Jess. She will need me. She'll be terrified.

I step out into the hall when I hear the words more clearly. "Fuck you, Chopper. I have nothing for you."

Chopper?

Daddy?

My legs buckle, and I grip the wall to stop myself falling. He's here? He's here, oh God. I take a step toward the stairs that lead up onto the deck. Can I do this? Can I see him again after all these years? It's been so long.

For so many years I dreamed about him, wanting him home. Can I face him now? Knowing he's likely a monster? I am doubting everything, and yet I'm still walking toward the stairs, like my body is refusing to accept those doubts.

The steps creak as I walk up them, and the yelling becomes more obscene and loud. When the sun shines into my eyes, I lift my hand, blocking it out. I peer over at the other ship lined up against Hendrix's. It's bigger, but older. There are more pirates, easily, and they look far scarier. There's a man in a dark, wide-brimmed hat, pointing a gun at Hendrix and snarling curses at him. He cocks his gun as I take a step, and I feel panic swell in my chest. Is he going to kill him?

"Stop!" I cry.

The man lifts his eyes to me and barks, "Who are you?"

My knees wobble, and I press a hand to my heart. It's him. I know that voice; I could never miss it. I open my mouth and croak out, "Daddy?"

He shakes his head, confused. "And you are?"

He doesn't recognize me. I walk closer, coming more clearly into his view. I know the moment he recognizes me, because the gun in his hand just slips and crashes onto the floor. He seems to sway on his feet, and his hand reaches up to tear his hat off his head.

"Indigo?" he rasps.

Tears leak from the corner of my eyes, and, step by wobbly step, I make my way closer. I see the years have been rather good to him, though his face holds a fair few scars. He's got thick blond hair that is down around his shoulders, and eyes that are sky blue. He's tall and broad, like he always was, only now he doesn't look fatherly—instead he looks like a pirate. Dark jeans, heavy boots, black shirt, and a gun belt slung around his waist.

"Daddy, is it really . . . ?"

I am about to step forward when I see a woman in the far corner of the ship, her eyes wide and frightened, her hands trembling. She looks terrified. It hits me like a brick then. My father buys women, and likely sells them. I make a strangled sound, and I watch as he turns his eyes to the girl. By the time he turns them back to me, I'm backing down the stairs.

"Indi!" he yells, reaching out his hand.

"You're . . . you left me and became a monster!" I cry. "You make women into sex slaves. You thought I was one . . . you were going to buy me . . . oh . . . God . . ."

"My daughter," he bellows, spinning to Hendrix and raising his gun. "You sick fuck."

"I didn't know she was your daughter," Hendrix barks.

"Hand her over, now, you fucking scumbag."

"Ain't gonna happen," Hendrix growls, lifting his gun.

"Stop!" I cry, running over and gripping Hendrix's arm. "I'm here by choice."

My dad turns his confused gaze to me. "What did you say?"

"I said, I'm here by choice."

"He was going to sell you!"

"And you were going to buy me!"

"Indi, just let me . . ."

"No!" I cry. "You left me, Daddy. You left me when I had nothing, and you never came back. Then I found out you were out here and using women as sex slaves . . ."

He curses under his breath, and then turns to his guys. "Lower your weapons. No one shoots while my daughter is on board."

"She remains on my ship, Charles," Hendrix growls.

My father turns his eyes toward mine. "I'm not welcome on your ship, just as you're not welcome on mine. The only thing that can move is her, and I wish to speak with her."

"She's not going on your ship. Over my dead fuckin' body."

"Stop it!" I cry, trembling. "Just leave me be."

"Indi!" my dad yells as I spin and rush toward the stairs. "I won't leave, princess. Not until you hear me out."

I block him out and rush below deck. I run into Jess, and she wraps her arms around me instantly. "I heard it all. I'm sorry, honey."

I say nothing, just walk with her to her room. Like many times before, we sit on her bed. I stare down at my hands, unsure how I feel. A huge part of me wants to run over and throw my arms around him, feeling his comfort. The other part is repulsed by thoughts of what he might have done.

"Are you okay?" Jess asks.

"I'm not sure," I whisper. "I don't know how I feel."

"Have you spoken to him?"

I shake my head. "It doesn't seem like he's going to leave until I do. They won't hurt each other because they're both protecting me. So they're just going to sit out there stewing until I decide what I want."

"Don't you want to talk to him?" Jess says gently.

"I do, but I'm scared of knowing. Hendrix was going to sell me to him, Jess. I'm not sure I can live with the reality of that, but . . ."

"But what?" she urges.

"I have so many questions."

"Can I say something?"

I nod, lifting my eyes to meet hers. "I know that part of you is scared to find out that your dad is a monster, but the fact he is waiting, desperate for you to hear him out, means he has a story to tell. Sometimes, as hard as things are to listen to, they give us closure. If you run now, and don't speak to him, you're going to spend your life wondering. I imagine it will hurt if your fears come true and he has done what you think, but isn't it going to be worse if you never know?"

She's right.

She's always right.

I reach across and grip her shoulders, hugging her close. "Thank you, Jess."

"You don't have to thank me."

I pull back. "You've risked your relationship with Hendrix for me. You've been by my side and helped me through so much."

She shrugs. "Helping people makes me happy, and I didn't risk anything with Hendrix . . . He still doesn't know it was me."

"I didn't think he did," I say quietly.

"Enough about me. Go up there, get your answers, and then start making the steps to create your life over again."

I nod, swallowing. "Thank you, Jess."

"Any time, sweetie."

I get up, and, with shaky legs, I head back toward the deck. Jess is right, I know she's right, but it doesn't make it any easier to process. I don't honestly know how I'll react if my father tells me that my worst fears are true, but I know I need closure. I at least need to know why he left.

I take each step slowly, one by one, taking deep breaths to keep my calm. I step out onto the deck, and I see Hendrix growling something at my father, who is leaning over the side of his ship growling something back.

My father notices me first, and he stands straight. "Indi . . ."

"I want to talk to you, but it isn't for your benefit. It's for mine," I say in a stern voice.

He nods.

Hendrix walks over, grips my shoulders, and leans down. "I'm not letting you on that ship, Indi."

"How do you suggest I talk to him, then?" I say back.

He lifts his head and glares at my father before looking down at me. "There is an island fifty miles south. We can stop. Mutual ground . . ."

"Sounds find to me," my father says.

"There's to be no fights, or I won't speak to either of you," I warn them.

"Understood," Hendrix mutters, but he doesn't look pleased about it.

"I'd never do that to you," my father says.

Hendrix snorts, and I glare up at him. "Stop it. I need to do this."

He lifts his head. "GG, sail us to the south island. We'll stop for the night."

"On it, Cap."

My father is staring at me, and it's hard for me to meet his gaze when he's looking at me like that. "I'll see you soon, princess," he murmurs, before walking off.

My entire body shivers, and I find a seat and slump down onto it. Hendrix falls down beside me, gripping my hand.

"You sure this is what you want, *inocencia*?"

"I'm sure," I whisper.

"You might not like what you hear."

"Tell me what you know, Hendrix."

He flinches a little, and then shakes his head. "It ain't my place, baby. You know that."

"When we first met, you said Chopper likes girls like me. Tell me what you meant."

He sighs. "He has a reputation of getting girls off people and selling them."

There has to be something we're not understanding here, something being left out. I just can't see him doing this.

"And you've sold him girls before?"

"No, but when I said I had a girl for him, as payment, he was more than willing to accept."

I swallow and look away as the two ships begin to move.

"I don't understand. I know my dad . . . It just doesn't fit . . ."

"He's a pirate, sweetheart."

"Would you sell girls?" I snap.

He tenses and narrows his eyes. "No, you know I wouldn't."

"Then you can't use being a pirate as an excuse for being a monster."

He stares at me a moment, then nods. "No, you're right, I can't."

I look out at the blue ocean, and close my eyes, breathing it in. My stomach is doing somersaults and my entire body is tense. I'm nervous, scared as hell, and desperate for answers. Hendrix wraps an arm around me and pulls me closer to him.

"It's going to be okay. No matter what, I've always got your back."

I hope he's right.

~

The island is equally as beautiful as the one we were on before. It's a little smaller, and the sand is more yellow than white, but the beach is just as stunning, the trees thick, the air fresh and pure. Both ships come to a complete stop a few hundred meters out. This island has little sand and more coral, so we have to pile into the lifeboats to get over to it. As soon as we all stop, I see my father jumping off his boat and striding toward me. I grip Hendrix's hand desperately.

"Got your back, baby," he murmurs. "I won't let anything happen to you."

"I'm frightened," I whisper.

"Indi," my father says when he stops.

Up close, I can see he has two scars on his face: one going up on an angle from his top lip, and the other up near his temple. His eyes search my face, and I can see so much emotion in them. He cares—even in all my fear I can see that. I look at Hendrix once more before nodding. My father turns, and together we walk off down the beach. When we're out of sight, he finds a spot on the sand and sits down. I do the same.

"I know how hard this is for you, Indigo . . ."

"No," I whisper, looking at my hands. "You don't."

"I do, because I, too, have had to live without the only thing I loved."

"You don't love me. You wouldn't have left if you loved me."

"I had no choice."

"There's always a choice," I cry, turning to him.

"No, princess, there isn't."

"Why did you go?" I ask, feeling my arms begin to shake.

"I did something, one night when I was out. I . . . killed someone."

I lift my head, feeling my eyes well with tears. "What?"

"It was an accident. I was drinking and decided to walk home. He came out of nowhere, and in my self-defense I went too far. I hit him so hard he went backward and landed on the footpath. He hit his head and was killed instantly. I knew what I had done, and I panicked. I couldn't spend the rest of my life in jail, so I did the only thing I could: I ran.

"I didn't become a pirate right away. I spent four years running, but one day I met a man in a bar. We got talking, and he told me stories of pirates and the laws on the ocean. Tired of running, I used what little money I had left to buy a ship. I've been out here since."

I'm crying now, big heavy sobs. My body trembles.

"Indi . . ." he whispers, reaching for me.

"Don't touch me!" I cry, slapping his hand away.

"I'm sorry. I know it means nothing to you now, but I am sorry."

"You left, for whatever reason, and you never came back. Not a call, not a card, nothing. Then Mom died and I got tossed through foster homes. I could have had you . . ."

"In jail," he says, his eyes hardening. "That's what would have happened. Your life wouldn't have been any easier."

I turn my face away, not wanting to admit that what he's saying is actually true.

"You were all I had," I whisper.

"I know," he says, his voice cracking. "Princess, I know."

"I need to . . . I need to know about the girls."

"The girls?" he asks, confused.

"The girls you sell."

He flinches when I meet his gaze. "I don't . . . shit . . . okay, princess, I don't sell them."

"Then you buy them and use them for yourself?" I rasp, trembling.

"No . . . I save them."

I blink, confused. "What?"

"Three years ago I was at a bar when we docked for a few nights. This girl came in. She was blond, blue-eyed, stunning. I kept an eye on her, I'm not even sure why, but she was getting around in this tiny dress and men were leering at her. She left at about midnight, and I noticed she walked out alone, very drunk. I followed her, just wanting to make sure she was safe. Anyway, this van pulled up beside her and before I knew what was happening, they were pulling her inside. I stood there and watched these men take her. Her face was all over the news for weeks, and after twelve months I saw that she had been found in a different country. Those men had sold her as a sex slave. I was sick at the thought that women were being targeted, so I got myself involved in the business. Most of the clients think I keep the women and sell them, but I send them home."

"Does Hendrix know this?" I rasp.

"No, no one does. The people who run these kinds of businesses aren't the kind of people you want to get on the wrong side of. They need to believe I am on their team, so to speak. Hendrix contacted me when he found you, and offered you as payment. I accepted, assuming that if I didn't take you, he'd sell you to someone else."

"Oh God," I whisper, rubbing my arms furiously.

"I might have done many things wrong in my time, Indigo, but I would never rape a woman, nor would I ever force her to be something she didn't want to be."

"That girl on your ship . . . she's . . . one of them, isn't she?"

"Yes, I picked her up three days ago from Mexico. I'm returning her home. She's extremely damaged. She's been without her family for three years."

Oh God, the poor thing. I couldn't imagine how it would feel to be so alone, so scared, and, mostly, so broken. I stare at the sand, trying to process everything. I honestly don't know how I feel. My father, he's all I have left, but he's also the enemy. I can't choose between the two, and I know a truce won't ever happen. I have to pick one, and I already know which one that will be. I need that one the most, no matter how much letting the other go will kill me.

"I love him, you know?" I say, lifting my head to meet his gaze.

"Hendrix?"

"Yes."

"He loves you too. I can see it."

"So you know . . . you know I choose him. I can't have a relationship with both of you. You're sworn enemies, and even if you can call a truce and leave each other alone, it's never going to be something that I can easily hop between."

"I know," he rasps. "I just . . . I just wanted to see you again, Indi. I wanted you to know that I love you, no matter what happened."

Tears slide down my cheeks, and I look away. "I love you too, Daddy. But I can't be in your life."

He makes a pained sound and reaches out, gripping my hand. I let him take it. My heart aches, because I know it's a decision I have to make, yet it doesn't make it any easier.

"Maybe one day . . . this will all be over, and we can see each other again."

"I'd like that," I rasp.

"I love you, Indi. Promise me you'll never forget that."

"I promise."

"And . . . I hope one day you can forgive me."

He gets to his feet and leans down, gripping the sides of my face and pressing his lips to my head. I close my eyes, holding back my sobs. When he pulls away, his eyes are glassy with emotion. He lets his gaze search my face once more before he turns and walks away.

When he's a few meters down the beach, I yell out to him. He stops and turns. I can't let him go without knowing that, no matter what, I forgive him. I get to my feet and rush over, throwing my arms around him.

He makes a strangled sound and wraps his big arms around me, holding me close. We stand like that for a long time, just hanging onto this moment. I lift my head from his chest and I look up at him. "I forgive you, Daddy."

I know those words heal something inside of him.

And surprisingly, they heal something inside of me, too. All these years, I have been searching for who I am. I've been thrown through homes, and been in relationships that were less than desirable, but I survived. I found someone who taught me something about myself, and somehow allowed me to put my heart back together. Not only that, but he allowed me to have this moment with my dad. They say everything happens for a reason, and I have finally realized that even though sometimes we don't know what that reason is, there always is one.

EPILOGUE

"Baby," Hendrix murmurs, running his fingers down the inside of my thigh. "Stop teasin' me."

"I'm not teasing you. It's right there for you, pirate," I grin.

"My point exactly: it's a damn tease."

I laugh softly as he runs his hand up and cups my pussy, using his palm to rub against it. "So damned sweet here."

"Best you make good use of it then, before it's not so sweet anymore."

He chuckles, and kisses a small path up my belly until he reaches my breasts. He slides his tongue out and makes little circles around my nipple. I whimper and drop my head into the pillow. He moves up, after gently caressing each breast, and finds my lips. He kisses me with need, sweeping his tongue into my mouth and stroking mine with it. His hands are all over me, touching and grasping. I writhe beneath him, lifting my legs and tucking them around his waist. He grinds his hips into mine, using that gentle thrusting motion that has everything coming alive.

We're just about to strip down when we hear an ear-piercing scream.

We both stop what we're doing and sit bolt upright. It sounds like Jess. We leap off the bed and straighten our clothes before rushing out the door. By the time we're above deck, the screaming seems to have gotten farther away.

I see a ship as soon as we step out. It's a newer ship, and it's a little smaller than Hendrix's, but it's definitely a pirate ship. We both rush toward the side, not seeing anyone for a moment, and then a tall man in a dark hood steps out, and he's holding Jess with a knife to her throat.

My heart stops.

How did he get her?

Was she on the deck? Did he just leap over and grab her?

"H . . . H . . . Hendrix," she whimpers, her face pale.

I clench my fists, feeling ill. Is he going to kill her? I can't even see his face. He steps closer to the edge, and when Hendrix lifts his gun, he growls and yells, "I wouldn't do that if I was you, pirate."

"Let her go," Hendrix growls.

"That's not going to happen. Not yet," he rasps.

"Who the fuck are you?"

The man laughs. "Didn't you hear there were new pirates on the block?"

"These are my fuckin' waters. Now I ask again: who the fuck are you?"

The man chuckles again. "Always thinking you own the world. Well, I'm here to show you that you don't."

"Give her back to me, or I'll blow your fucking brains out," Hendrix growls.

"Oh, her?" the man says, pressing the knife closer to Jess's throat. "No, I think I will keep her a while."

"What do you fuckin' want?" Hendrix barks, raising his gun.

"You shoot me, she dies. I won't hesitate."

"Don't," I whisper as Hendrix's hands begin to tremble. "One wrong move and she dies. You can't risk her Hendrix. Please."

"If a fight is what you want, I'll give it to you," Hendrix hisses, lowering his gun.

"Oh, I want a fight, don't you worry about that, but I want so much more first. I want you to suffer. I'm going to take this girl, and I'm going to make her suffer. Every moment she's with me, you're going to know it's your fault. You're going to drown inside, and you're going to begin going mad. Then you're going to come and find me, and when you do, I'll be ready. She's going to give me every bit of information you've ever given her, and I am going to make sure I destroy you in the worst, most painful way possible. See, if I just kill you now, I won't be satisfied. You need to suffer first. I've been wanting this for so long you can't even begin to imagine the kind of fucked up I am."

I watch with wide eyes as the man reaches up and grips his hood, lowering it. I gasp, one, because he's much younger than I imagined, and two, he's devastating. I'm not talking beauty. I'm talking pure, raw, masculinity—the kind that makes you want to drop to your knees and lick him from head to toe. He has dark hair that sits around his shoulders, and, by the looks of it, it's thick and silky. His eyes are light—from this distance I can't tell just how light, but I can see they are. His body is tall, extremely powerful, and, from the glimpse of his shoulder peeking through the coat, ripped. He has that overly masculine square jaw, a straight nose, and big, full lips. He's absolutely mind-blowing to look at.

I hear Hendrix gasp beside me, and I turn to see him locking eyes with the young man.

"Did you really think I'd never come back for my revenge?" the young man rasps.

"If you're here for revenge, take it out on me, not her," Hendrix hisses.

"See, that's where you're not seeing the big picture." The younger man grins, pressing the knife closer. Jess cries out. "This is all for you."

"You're wrong about everything," Hendrix says, his voice becoming gentler. "If you'll just . . ."

"Shut the fuck up," the young man roars. "Don't fucking tell me your bullshit lies."

He takes a step back and lifts a hand, waving it. The ship begins to move.

"Jess!" I cry. "Hendrix, you can't let him take her."

Jess is still trembling. Her eyes are wide and frightened.

"You want the girl back alive?" the young man bellows. "Then you fight for her."

The ship keeps moving back, and we both stand in shock. Hendrix turns suddenly, screaming out for his boys. Some are already on deck, guns raised, but at his call the rest appear.

"Not wise," the young man yells, and then whistles. A moment later at least forty pirates appear, all armed, all deadly.

There's no way Hendrix has the men, or the weapons, to fight them. They're holding guns I've never seen in my life, and they look deadly.

"Back away, or I slit her throat and then my men destroy you."

Hendrix waves a hand, and everyone lowers their weapons. He can say nothing; he just watches in shock. The young man laughs. "See you soon, Hendrix."

"Hendrix?" I whisper, gripping his arm, hearing my own voice tremble. "Who is that?"

"That is Dimitri," he rasps. "My stepson."

I grip his hand, and he trembles. "Is she going to be okay? Tell me for real, Hendrix."

He looks mortified. "I don't know. I really don't know."

As we watch the ship disappear into the distance I know we're both praying that we can find a way to get Jess out of this.

One thing we both know is we will fight to the end for her.

THE END

I know, I know, I've left you with a little cliffhanger, but really, it's just an entry into Jess and Dimitri's story. Their book will be explosive, and dark, and amazing. You will see more of Hendrix and Indi in their story, so don't panic! Much love, my sweets.

ACKNOWLEDGEMENTS

There are so many people I'd like to thank for the help in writing this book. The first of those is my amazing Beta Reader Sali. For being with me every step of the way when writing this and throwing some seriously good pirate jokes at me. You made this real for me.

I'd love to thank the team from Montlake Publishing for giving this book a chance – I dared to do something different and you believed in me. You've been amazing to work with. It's such an honor.

To my loyal and loving fans – of course I couldn't have made it this far without you. Thank you for always reading and always believing.

Most of all, thank you to my beautiful family. For it's pirates that started me on this journey and it's pirates that made my dreams come true. Without all of you, I could have never believed I was worth.

ABOUT THE AUTHOR

Bella Jewel is an Australian author. She's a twenty-six-year-old mother to two children. Writing isn't something she ever planned on doing, but there isn't a moment that goes by now that she isn't sitting with book ideas running through her mind. She loves the Australian bush, and calls Far North Queensland her home. She spends her weekends with her family swimming in local creeks and having a good laugh.

Printed in Great Britain
by Amazon